Southpaw

Short Stories

Lisa St Aubin de Terán

A *Virago* Book

Published by Virago Press 1999

A CIP catalogue record for this book
is available from the British Library

ISBN 1 86049 532 X

Typeset in Bembo by M Rules
Printed and bound in Great Britain
by Clays Ltd, St Ives plc

Virago Press
A Division of
Little, Brown and Company (UK)
Brettenham House
Lancaster Place
London WC2E 7EN

Contents

Introduction

This collection of short stories was written over a period of twenty-five years. Some, like *Eladio and the boy* and *Zapa, the fire child*, were part of my first book, *Keepers of the House* (which began life as a series of short stories on a theme), but were then excluded to streamline the contents. With the exception of *Dom Leopoldo*, which is set in Brazil and was inspired by the great Latin American classic, *Pedro Paramo*, all the South American stories are set on or around the Hacienda Santa Rita, the sugar plantation in the Venezuelan Andes where I lived and worked between 1972 and 1979.

All the characters in the hacienda stories are based on real characters, dead or alive, but then roam out into the realms of fantasy as all stories do there in their recounting. Some of the stories were written at night in my study in The Big House on the hacienda, others were written in Italy remembering it.

The title, *Southpaw*, reflects the awkward, unexpected elements of these South Americans; each a survivor, each a fighter in his or her own way, and each both dogged and shaped by their different approach to life within the narrow parameters of the rules of their ring. As in boxing, their excellence is shown as much in their ability to receive blows as to administer them and the rarity of their southpaw punch obliges their opponents to adapt their own strategies in the fight.

The latter part of this collection are all stories set in Italy. Like the earlier South American ones, they evolve around a small, isolated rural community in which I have chanced to live and chosen to become enmeshed.

The fields around our small Umbrian village are planted mostly with tobacco. There is no sugar cane there or tropical plants. But the lore and legend, the customs and even the landscape that surround it are in many ways reminiscent of my years on the hacienda, as are the sounds of the cicadas bleating through hot summer nights. Just as the place and people in the Andes became a mainspring of my writing, they have come to be so in Italy. In each, I am an alien observer. In each, in the absence of anywhere else to specifically claim as home, I have found an emotional home in other people's roots.

All the Italian stories were written over the last ten years. They have grown out of an oral tradition (like so much of my work), centring around the quirky southpaws of another south. *Antonio Mezzanotte* is the least fictional of them all, being the factual account it purports to be. After writing *Nocturne*, a novel drawn from the seed of the Mezzanotte story, the true character kept thanking me for having told the story of his life. The novel is a fantasy, the short story here is a homage to Antonio Mezzanotte himself.

Dom Leopoldo

I wondered what the line would be like without the heat, but I couldn't imagine it. I'd been on the train from Campo Grande for eight hours, stopping and starting, needing a drink and needing a shave. My new suit was stuck to the plastic covering of my seat. I was sweating like all the other passengers and, like them, swatting mosquitoes against the sides of the carriage.

I knew the stations – Ribas do Rio Pardo, Mutum, Garcias, Tres Lagoas, and all the others en route to Taveiras. The train was taking me through the tracks of my childhood; not because I have ever been away from the town where I was born, but the names were all on the timetable that faded from year to year on the noticeboard beside the lavatory shed that it was my mother's job to keep clean. Passing through them, I was aware of having expected them to smell of urine and disinfectant and diarrhoea, and I was surprised that they didn't. Beyond that, I knew that I had no other expectations for my journey. I was heading for Taveiras and nothing else could interest me. So I passed through the Mato Grosso do Sul like a ghost. It was only outside Garcias, passing a cemetery with its blue tombstones and crosses that

I felt a chill, and that was when I tried to imagine how it would be without the heat. When I was a boy, an ice lorry turned over in our street and we rolled in the cold blocks. There was no ice on the train though, and my childhood had gone with its last string cut by my mother's death.

I already knew Taveiras, as I knew the places that led to it, secondhand. My mother had left her village carrying me in her womb, and she never returned, but she had pined for it, for the two bars on opposite corners of the main street, for the pumping station with its cattle fence, for the avenue of jacaranda trees, for Rosaria's miraculous mango tree with its thousands of kilos of ripe fruit that fell like a carpet overnight, burying the ground around it knee deep in orange sludge. I knew the schoolhouse with its four windows and sky-blue shutters painted at the end of the rainy season by the children in the top grade, and I felt I knew the peeling shutters and the shacks of every cane-cutter and cattle-herder whose huts lined the long street that stretched out from the centre of Taveiras, from the station.

My mother's name was Nelida Cardosa. She was old and thin and her hands smelled of creosote. The doctor who signed her death certificate asked me her age and I was ashamed not to know it. She had a friend, an engine driver from Agua Clara who sometimes came to lunch. Each time he came, my mother would send me out to strangle one of our hens, which made him a special friend. He was sixty last year and his elder brother drank himself to death at the birthday party.

'How old is your mother?' the doctor had asked me.

4

'Sixty,' I lied, thinking of her friend.

The doctor had little use for our street and no respect for my grief. He cuffed me round the side of my head and sent me reeling, 'What sort of shit did they teach you in school, you useless thing . . . Look at her! She can't be a day over forty!'

I looked at her wasted corpse on the high iron bed. She looked old and thin. She looked older than her friend and older than the drunk. She looked shrivelled and grey and I wanted the doctor to take her away.

That was when I realised that I knew all the people from her village, her mother, her father, her sisters and her friends, but I didn't really know her. I had grown up beside her in our one dark room; I had carried cans of kerosene for the stove, fetched rice and yucca, waited for her at the station while she finished her work, helped her sometimes to swill out the corrugated iron cabin with one hole in the floor for men, one for women. I had mended the wire catch of the doors innumerable times. I had memorised the timetables from Miranda to Bauru. I knew the dates of all the worst derailments and crashes along the line, but I didn't know either her birthday or her saint's day and I didn't know her age; I only knew mine: I was nineteen.

As the train moved nearer to Taveiras, I tried to remember all I could of my mother, partly for me, and partly to be able to give some account of her to her family. Perhaps they would not accept me if they realised how little I knew of the thin woman who had raised me. She loved green things; she kept a shrine of flowers by the window of our room. She grew plants in milk tins and they trailed into each other. Sometimes she seemed to live in a trance; in the evenings, after her work was done, she would sit for hours with her hands in her lap, ironing out the creases of her print frock with her palms, staring into the darkness without paying any attention to the chorus of radios from along the street or the cries or fights from other rooms. Sometimes the day would end like that and I would eat whatever food I could scavenge from the wooden box that served as a kitchen to us. Sometimes, though, my mother would begin to speak into the twilight or the night like a travelling storyteller, imposing her voice, raising it slowly until it could be heard above the background noises. Hers was an incantation of nostalgia, a telling of years and faces. My mother could talk for hours like that. I think she noticed when I stayed by her and listened to her tales. I think she wanted me to know. It was a subject she never brought up later and nor did I. I would have liked to ask questions. If her father had a special boot weighted with stones which he wore at the end of his leg where his own foot was missing, I wanted to know how he lost his foot. Was it an accident in the cane fields, a fight, or a snake bite? And if so many women in Taveiras carried a black mark on their face criss-crossed with lines like the lines of destiny, a black growth on their cheek, why didn't she have one? She called it the devil's cross; but why? And why had she left her village and sought out the loneliness of our lives? And why did she blend such bitterness in her voice with that hint of happiness, almost passion; an elusive quality lost to all but her potplants and her stews of boiled fowl and occasionally a pull at my arm which was the nearest she ever came to affection? A gecko was trapped in the compartment, staring warily down at the lethargic passengers. I had been watching its tiny transparent hands, willing it to approach me. It did, darting towards my window. I grabbed it, neatly dividing its body into head and tail. When I threw the head out of the window, it was still staring. Its hands waved like a child's. Once, remembering still my mother's ways, our room was so plagued by heat I couldn't swallow my supper and I took my tin plate of beans out into the yard to eat under the relative cool of the sun without the intervening pressure of our corrugated iron roof. We shared our yard with three other families who filled it so totally; eating, sleeping, making love, fighting and gossiping there, that our only claim to it really was as a scrabbling place for our five hens. That day, I remember, the yard was empty; there was fever in the neighbourhood and fever round our yard. I was seven or eight and used to being shouted at by all and sundry, but my mother had a gentle voice which she kept to herself, rationing her use of words as though saving them for her occasional monologues. I learnt what I could and couldn't do by instinct and by watching closely to see what would and wouldn't please. Usually we ate on our laps in our room, but that day I strolled out with my plate. The next thing I knew it was knocked from my hands and the chickens were eating my beans.

'Don't ever let me see you eating in the yard!' my mother screamed at me and dragged me back inside.

Pedrinho Urupes had died in that yard, why couldn't I eat there? I never had the courage to ask her. I never really asked her anything, not even her age.

Before she was taken ill, one rainy season when the whole town was swallowed up by noise and mud and mildew crept over everything including our feet, she pined more than ever for her family. She talked night after night about her friend Teresa from Taveiras, about missing her and wondering how she was. I thought I'd found a chink in her loneliness. I had noticed that when the refugees poured in from the villages to Campo Grande, looking for work and hiding from hunger, their friends and relatives followed them via the station-master. Anyone could receive letters at the station and there were stalls at the market where scribes could be paid to write back, once again, to whoever it was, care of the station-master of whatever village in the outback.

Given our penury and her loneliness, I thought we too could write, care of the station-master at Taveiras. I suggested it. She took the wooden cross down from above her bed and made me kiss it, 'Promise me, on my life and on this cross that you will never contact the station-master of Taveiras. Never. Dom Leopoldo has nothing to do with our lives!'

I promised, but I remembered. Dom Leopoldo was the one name she had never mentioned from her past, from which, rightly or wrongly, I deduced that he was my father. From that moment, secretly, I felt drawn to that place. I had asked when I was too young to know better, 'Who was my father?'

8

'You never had a father,' she would say and turn away from me as though threatening me with the loss of my mother too if I were to insist.

Dom Leopoldo was a grand name, as grand as a car or a cinema, as grand as a new saddle or a house with a balcony. My promise died with my mother. Without her job I had no money; my own work was seasonal and I had recently been laid off. I had enough to buy myself a one-way ticket to Taveiras and enough to keep myself in bread and drink for a while. The rest was a dream of Dom Leopoldo and whatever fortune or future he might give me. At worst, I thought, he can give me a job in a place where I belong.

I had to keep changing trains. I didn't mind, I wasn't in any hurry. I had waited nineteen years to go home. I waited on the wooden benches of dusty stations along the way, sipping guaranà fizz and watching the girls go by with their bundles of goods and babies. Everywhere I stopped, I noticed the station-master was the grandest person around. His uniform was fit for a military band, his braids shone in the sun. At Val Paraiso, since I had to wait for some time, I got talking to a little boy naked from the waist up but as fat and glistening as the babies I'd seen in the air-conditioned trucks parked outside the stores on the main street in Campo Grande, babies from another breed. Such a one was the little boy who sat with me, shifting his rolls of flesh from side to side as he informed me that he was the station-master's son.

9

I talked to him eagerly, happily, imagining future steaks and ice-creams heading my way as they must have done his. At one point I was aware of the station-master himself coming towards us, ready to shoo his boy away back to the protection of his own. But, seeing me treat the child so respectfully, he halted the curse that was halfway out and asked me my business instead.

'I see you didn't want the express to Bauru so you can't be heading there or on to São Paolo, but you look lost, where are you heading?'

'I'm on my way to Taveiras.'

'Indeed!' he said, and laughed. 'You say it, you know, as though announcing that you were on your way to the court of the Emperor Dom Pedro.' He paused and pulled his son to him, stroking the boy's bare shoulder with pride. 'I almost thought you were about to announce that you had business with the Emperor of Taveiras, with Dom Leopoldo himself.'

I didn't know what to say. I was caught unawares and blushed like a girl.

'People used to come through this station looking for Dom Leopoldo, but no one ever came through without carrying a gun, and no one ever came back again. There's a prize cock for you: he won his spurs.' Having said this, the station-master turned on his heel, and left me not knowing what to make of his speech.

After all my hundreds of miles of track, there was no train for Taveiras from Aracatuba that I could make out for days. My impatience was burning me up. I made my way around the town, telling anyone who would hear me that I was Nelida Cardosa's son on my way home with a message for Dom Leopoldo. My mother was unknown there, which didn't surprise me, she'd been gone nineteen years and I had no evidence that she had ever been out of the village before. There was no reason why she should be known in the town, but I had thought that it would be enough to cross the plain and bear the heat and say her name for a family to gather round me and draw me in. I couldn't give up, I had nowhere else to go and no other dream beyond Taveiras. So I insisted, and through the name of the man I wanted to be my father, I found myself a ride in an ox cart.

'Dom Leopoldo!' the carter told me. 'There's a name to reckon with. I fear no good will come from carrying messages to him. You'd do better to go back to this Nelida.'

'She's dead,' I told him.

He tipped his straw hat and dipped his head towards the floor of the cart and grunted.

'I see. Well, I see too that you have the look of Dom Leopoldo about you. Perhaps you are one of his sons?'

'Did he have so many then?'

'As many as there are hairs on a stick of cane.'

'And did he recognise any of them?'

'Dom Leopoldo said once to the whole gathered village of Taveiras that he was the biggest bastard in the world and therefore he'd be hard put to share his own bastardry with any others, but once a year, all his bastard sons were welcome to come and eat in his yard.'

'And did they?'

'Certainly, all hoping for a part of the Leopoldo inheritance; you see, Dom Leopoldo made money hand over
fist. Tariffs here and his own taxes there, protection money
and levies, there was a time you couldn't raise your head
around these parts without finding the heel of Dom
Leopoldo's boots on your throat and his hand held out for
money.'

The carter drove on, with his painted wooden cart
bumping along the dusty road between an avenue of high
sugar cane feathered grey above. The red earth rose and
settled into my skin, but I was not displeased; I thought of
it as a baptism of dust, a mark of being part of the place.

Remembering my mother's so recent death, I felt suddenly guilty to be sitting beside an old man rocking and
jolting in such contentment as he unravelled the very
stories I longed to hear. I had acquired a new skin of red
dust, a film that covered my city clothes (for I had dressed
smartly for my journey) and underneath it I was changing
like a snake ready for its next season. The carter smiled at
me and I smiled back as though from a great height, it was
the height of the one son who had never waited in Dom
Leopoldo's yard. I began to feel that my father was waiting
for me and had been waiting for me for years. I wished I
had my own horse and some fine Bauru boots and a hat
and a pair of silver pistols to ride into Taveiras with, rather
than that worm-eaten cart. But, as the road passed and my
eyes clogged up with dust, I felt the grit on my teeth and
I felt that Dom Leopoldo would recognise me no matter
how I came. Nothing that the carter told me of my

father's meanness did anything but inflate his image in my mind. I was jolted from my trance by the carter nudging me.

'This is Taveiras,' he said. 'I'm driving on, this is your last chance to ride on with me. Whatever nonsense you have in your head, no good can come of it.' I shook my head and clambered down, thanking him. Instead of any further words, he crossed himself and drove on.

The street was less than I had expected. It was unpaved, a dirt road. But it was lined, as my mother had told me, with huge jacaranda trees. I stood staring into them for so long that when I looked around the carter had gone. I wondered how he could have left so quickly and without leaving a cloud of dust, but I had no time to think about it more because a dog had come to worry me and seemed set on biting off one of my new shoes.

Not three paces behind me, by the side of the road, a woman was sitting shelling beans into a chipped basin. Her fingers kept opening the dried pods, but her eyes were staring at me in such a way that I could not tell whether or not it was in welcome.

'Good day,' I called to her.

'Eh!' she either answered or coughed.

'I am the son of Nelida Cardosa,' I told her, calling still despite being near enough to touch her.

'Are you indeed!' she said. 'I knew Nelida . . . it must be twenty years since she took the train . . .'

The woman was sitting on an upturned oil drum with her legs apart and her lap full of beans, her skin was a strange shade of grey, highlighted by a raised mole on her left cheek.

'I, too, had child by him,' she told me.

'By . . .?' I knew whom she meant but I wanted to hear it spoken and acknowledged.

'Am I to believe your mother never spoke of Dom Leopoldo?'

I kept my silence, hoping to draw her out and also to conceal how little I knew about him.

'Surely you know how he loves calamity? He thrives on it! He'd get the poor crippled boy who served him to polish his spurs every time a field crop failed or a stream burst its banks and flooded a hut or plot of yucca. Dom Leopoldo would pace up and down the platform with his panama hat pulled forward and his riding crop in his hand waiting like the vulture he is.'

The dog had taken up guard beside her, following her words as though he understood them all, with his skeletal rib cage heaving. For a moment she stopped both her story and her shelling and smiled up at me, a broad toothless smile.

'I am Nelida's aunt, Maria Cardosa. Come closer.' She beckoned me to sit on a log beside her. I sat down and a tightness in my chest made me feel suddenly far away and alone. I wanted to stand again and see the devil's cross on her face for comfort, but her big rough hand waved me back to my log.

'Dom Leopoldo gives tickets away on his trains, tickets to the cities; but they are never free. The girls have to pay for them in favours. He keeps a bed behind the ticket office. He keeps a busy station. He makes no secret of it. Daughters, fiancées, wives, widows, he boasts of them all. What isn't given willingly is taken by force. He used to be a man without any weakness, and then, to everyone's surprise, he developed a weakness for Nelida. He began to court her, to send flowers and coffee and frocks. He sent her a heifer and a fine black mare. She was fourteen, she was shy, she had been poorly as a child and rarely went beyond the confines of her house which was why he'd never seen her before. Perhaps he fell for her because she was the only girl in the village untainted by his bad ways.

'At night, he serenaded her, standing in the middle of the street with his guitar and a heap of songs I'd never heard before. The more Nelida ignored him, the more he took it out on the rest of the village.

'For two years he courted her. He offered her all that he owned to share; his sugar plantation, the estate house, his corral of horses. He offered her fine clothes, a cart to drive in, a life of ease if she would only acknowledge his love.'

'Why didn't she then?' I had to ask, seeing my birthright retrospectively squandered.

'Nelida hated him, and when she saw him weaken she despised him. She would laugh in his face. When he came to our house, she would refuse to see him. Her father beat her for it, but she didn't care, she took pleasure in defying Dom Leopoldo.'

'But in the end . . .?'

'Ah, in the end, as you can see, you are here and Nelida is dead.'

I was surprised that this woman could know of my mother's death so soon after the event; none but the carter had known and he had not paused to pass on any news. She looked into my eyes, almost, it seemed, defying me to ask her about it. I felt vertigo. I kept my peace. She ran her hand through the beans in her lap and I fancied they were a pile of maggots. She smiled again and tipped them all on to the ground where the dog began to nuzzle them.

'I have things to do,' she said abruptly. 'Come back later. If you're looking for the station house it's that way, by the garden.'

I followed her directions. A humming bird had settled on an acacia blossom at the edge of a tangle of flowers. I looked in and saw a confusion of colours and my nostrils filled with the scent of jasmine. The garden was overgrown, it had the look of somewhere that is sporadically tended. Lacing over most of the other plants was a trellis of morning glories. I walked along the wicket fence to its gate, turning off the main road. Ahead of me, I saw the pumping station with its high barbed-wire fence. To my left there was a run-down shed, to my right, the gate, more garden and a station house fronted by a platform.

I climbed on to the platform and made my way straight to the ticket office window. Above its arched aperture was a painted sign, but inside was a heap of empty rum and cachaza bottles. I looked around me trying to get my bearings. Beyond the platform was the track with the railway lines

16

stretching out north and south through banks of high grass and wild cane. Strung between its posts and signals was a rope washing line with a few tattered clothes flayed by the sun.

There were several doors, heavy, ornate wooden doors, but they all seemed closed and the heat and rain had beaten them to a uniform cracked grey. From inside, I could hear the familiar hum of a radio. I knocked on the biggest of the doors. Nobody answered, so I knocked again and waited. I could hear the tree frogs around me and the cicadas whining into the twilight; I had not noticed the sun going down. I knocked again and called out. I could hear breathing on the other side of the door and someone had turned the radio down.

'I am Nelida Cardosa's son,' I said. 'I have come from Campo Grande, I have a message for the station-master.'

'We don't take messages,' a woman's voice informed me.

'I'm Nelida Cardosa's son,' I repeated. 'She's dead.'

The door opened a crack and a broad black face looked me over. A woman opened the door and then turned her back and lumbered away into another room. I went in cautiously and found myself alone with an old man propped on a chair in a corner between two doorways. He had grizzled white hair and his hands were resting on a walking stick. His eyes stared at me but they were blind and pale blue with cataracts.

'Have you eaten?' the woman asked me.

'No, but I'm not hungry, thank you.'

'Eat,' she said, and shuffled around behind me in a

makeshift kitchen. She served me a plate of beans. I sat
down, relieved to be accepted, but puzzled by the mixture
of railway things and her own inhabitation of the station
building.

'I was looking for Dom Leopoldo.'

'He isn't here. He'll be back with the rains. He always
comes back with the rains. Carlos and I make do here, as
you can see, but it isn't easy now that everyone has gone
from Taveiras.' She brought me a glass of sugar-cane juice
and pushed it across the formica table to me, slopping some
as she did so. I noticed that she too bore the devil's cross on
her cheek with its grey-edged fissures weaving a pattern on
the growth.

'I've been talking to Maria Cardosa,' I told her, hoping to
get her talking again.

'Maria Cardosa died fifteen years ago at the edge of the
road. She died like a dog. What did she have to say?'

'She was shelling beans,' I told her.

'Carlos was soft on her once. After she died, he wanted
Dom Leopoldo to do something for her daughter. It took
him a long time to pluck up the courage.' She lowered her
voice. 'It's only really since he lost his sight that he's felt
man enough to confront him. You see, he doesn't fear what
he can't see . . . unlike some.' I looked out towards the
waiting-room and old Carlos in his corner.

'So he's waiting for Dom Leopoldo too?'

'Well; he says he's waiting for the train, but it's more the
man he's waiting for. He always comes back with the rains.'

'And when will the train come? Some of the timetables

18

along the way had trains to Taveiras four times a week, but when I tried to get one at Aracatuba the station-master told me he couldn't tell when there'd be another.'

'That's been the trouble here for years, those changing timetables. Teresa Ruiz, your mother's friend, used to walk along the tracks sometimes, she said it tempted the trains off from the junction. She was never very sound in the head, that one. Not that she was the only one to walk the tracks; you see, the railway lines are a clear road through the undergrowth, you get less mud and less snakes and less dust in the heat. We've all walked along them in our time.'

The woman moved her unwieldy body through the kitchen, brushing past Carlos who swayed in his seat but said nothing. She continued talking to me, but her voice trailed so I got up and followed her; she'd gone into a room beyond the waiting-room. It had high rafters hung with cobwebs. There was a large desk in the middle of the room, an imposing solid piece with many drawers. On either side, against the walls, were two beds.

'Where's the ticket office?' I asked her, interrupting her dirge for the order of things past. She pointed towards a pile of clutter shored up against a narrow door.

'It's through there, this is Dom Leopoldo's office. He used to have five or six men working here, but now there's only Carlos. After your mother left Taveiras, Dom Leopoldo lost himself in rum. He was drinking two or three bottles a day. He let his affairs go, his estate, his crops, his horses they all went to ruin. He didn't seem to care so long as he was at liberty to wander around moping after

Nelida Cardosa. I've heard him at night weeping like a woman for the return of that girl.'

She paused to think, muttering under her breath and counting on her fingers. 'She'd be thirty-five about by now, that's a long time to love someone when you think about it.'

I could think of nothing else, my head was entirely filled with this talk of my mother and her suitor. I tried to imagine how the thin person I had known, the shadowy voice, could have inspired such passion.

'I want to see Dom Leopoldo now,' I blurted out. 'What's all this nonsense about waiting for the rains? It's nearly two months still till then. Tell me where I can find him, please.'

The woman walked past me again, knocking into me slightly as though she were drunk or had no sense of balance. She wasn't drunk though, I could tell.

'Where is he?'

'Who can tell, I can't tell you, I don't know. He'll come back with the rains. As to the rest, there was a time when he could be found passed out with rum on the railway tracks, but that was a long time ago. Where are any of the people from around here? . . . My own children, where have they gone?'

She shuffled out across the waiting-room casting her eyes around the wooden benches fixed to the walls as though hoping to retrieve some of her lost sons there. The air was oppressive inside. The heat of the day had eased but it was far from cool and I felt suddenly as though she had mixed dust and cobwebs into my beans. I told her I was going out for some fresh air.

'Will you be back?' she asked anxiously. 'They don't come back, you see. Come back and wait with Carlos, it will be company for me.' I told her I'd return, 'We're cousins,' she shouted after me, 'on your mother's side.'

I walked back down to Maria Cardosa's shack. In the place where it had been, there was nothing but a small wooden cross stuck into a clump of weeds. Time and place were playing tricks on me. Perhaps I was just tired. I paced along the edge of the dirt road under the canopy of jacaranda, but no matter how I searched, there was no trace either of a hut or of Maria Cardosa herself, only the cross. I made a last foray beyond the village, skirting back in through a street of abandoned cottages and shacks. It seemed that the woman at the station house was right, all the people of Taveiras had gone.

I was no longer looking for Maria Cardosa when I saw her again looking as alive as anyone I had ever seen. She was sitting on the very edge of the road again, shelling beans in the night with a cloud of fireflies lighting up her face.

'So you've come back.'

I sat down beside her.

'Are you afraid?' she asked kindly.

I was afraid but I wasn't going to say so, instead I began to stroke the creases of my ruined city suit with the palms of both my hands, working at the cloth as my mother used to do. I shook my head.

'I want to find Dom Leopoldo.'

'Didn't they tell you at the station house? He'll be on the line, face down in the tracks before you reach the junction on the way to Aracatuba. I've always heard that he mistreated his own mother, so if I say that he's wallowing for the only woman he ever loved that's no exaggeration. He's been pining for Nelida ever since she left. The man who took the entire neighbourhood by force and who thought it his right to rape every woman he could lay his hands on has never forgiven himself for forcing your mother. It has been his undoing.'

I thanked Maria and left her, not daring to look back to see if I should find a woman or a wooden cross behind me. Then I made my way through the night towards the tracks. The moon was almost full and, together with the fireflies, I was no more aware of the dark than I would have been by the light of a lamp. Outside the station house the tracks shone as though they had been newly polished by a passing train, and the sleepers were weeded and clean. I walked along them, picking my way across their regular ladder.

Almost immediately beyond the platform, the grass and weeds had begun to grow and the tracks and sleepers were strangled with creepers. Between the slabs of wood, canes and thorn bushes had grown up making it hard to follow the line at all. I wished I had a machete with me to cut my way through. I realised there that whatever any timetables or people said, no train had passed this way for some years. I kept going, lured by the hope of finding Dom Leopoldo further on, expecting to find some kind of shelter there where my deranged father might be squatting. The mesh of weeds continued and then stopped giving way to a stretch of railway line no more than ten yards long. Here, the sleepers themselves were clear of undergrowth but rotting in their slots. The metal rails were rusted and buckled.

It was dank without there being any signs of water and chill on that warm night. In the middle, I saw something lying: two objects on the slimy wood. I knelt down to inspect them, and felt myself held, by a power that was beyond me, to stay in that attitude of prayer, ruining my best trousers once and for all on the rotting wood. Before me was a cracked and discoloured panama hat and a raw hide riding crop The hat bore the strange criss-crossing of a Taveiras growth.

After I don't know how many moments, I picked up the hat and crop and took their crumbling rotting remains back in my two hands. Before leaving that place, I saw that further on the weeds began again, but the railway line had come to an end.

Back at the station house, my cousin was waiting for me.

'You should have waited here,' she said.

I put the bits of hat and crop down on one of the benches in the waiting room. She nodded towards them.

'No one wanted to touch them after it happened.'

'What happened?'

'He was drunk on the track. He used to know what days were safe and what were not, but he'd let everything go by then. They said they sent word down the line, letters and things with the new timetable, changing the days; because really it wasn't every day there were trains here, it was more the traffic of girls than other goods that made their way through this station. So, he didn't know about the new timetable and he was sprawled out there, calling out to Nelida in his sleep no doubt, when the train came and drove straight over him.'

I thought, there is some trick here, some plot to rob me of my inheritance.

'Aha! How then can Dom Leopoldo come back with the rains?'

'He always does, he always has. Taveiras is a strange place. Didn't your mother tell you how strange it is?'

I thought of Rosaria Bello's mango tree with its carriage loads of fruit falling overnight. That was the nearest my mother had ever come to telling me of miracles or the mixing of the living and the dead. For the rest, she had talked so much and told me so little, all I knew of her past from her was that her name was Nelida Cardosa of Taveiras.

Old Carlos was staring out with his blind eyes to where the moonlight reflected on the tracks.

'How come you have stayed on here when all the rest of the villagers have gone?'

'Carlos has some business with Dom Leopoldo and then, we've nowhere else to go.'

For the third time that day, she pushed past me.

'Have you eaten?'

'No, I'm not hungry.'

24

'Eat!' she said and pushed another plate of her cobwebby beans across the table.

Outside and all across the surrounding cane fields, the cicadas seemed to be chanting my name, but whether it was because I had come or my mother had gone I couldn't tell. When I had eaten my beans, my cousin leant over towards me and put her face near mine. 'Will you be waiting for a while? There's an extra bed for you, Carlos never leaves his corner.'

'I have some business with Dom Leopoldo and then . . . I've nowhere else to go,' I told her, turning my mouth away from hers so as not to have to wonder about the cold wind of her breath.

Death of a purist

Alfredo Peña didn't come from the Barrio, but he'd settled there like a rare object caught in the silt of one of the many annual landslides that the rains brought down the slope and deposited in the Barrio, which was built on the hill unasked and unwanted. During the dry season, the debris from the rains was covered with weeds; some took root enough to withstand the inevitable deluge to follow, and some were washed away. Alfredo Peña dropped roots that no one could discover, and stayed there.

The streets of the Barrio were made of dirt, the huts were made of anything that could be wedged together with mud and, occasionally, cement. There were rooms made out of crates and corrugated iron, and rooms made out of the chassis of abandoned cars. Canes from the river banks were tied and bound by mud which caked in the sun. Every year, dozens of shacks were washed away, but the rest remained and gained a permanence in the shanty town.

Alfredo Peña was different from all his neighbours in so many ways that it was hard to know where to start the list. Perhaps, the most obvious difference was that, whereas everyone else wanted only to get out of the Barrio, Alfredo had gone against the social tide and chose to dig his way in. He was oblivious to squalor. The lack of drains or sanitation, the lack of electricity, the compacted rubbish that lay ankle-deep in the streets, the stench of decomposing chickens and dead dogs never impinged on his life. Day by day, he stepped absent-mindedly over the Pepsi-Cola tins and the feathers, the broken glass and the litter on his way in and out of his patchwork shack.

Unlike the other huts where people lived open to the prying eyes of those who already knew the business of every derelict, beggar, prostitute and invalid who lived there, and who knew the trials and triumphs of every bare-foot grubby child born to the Barrio, Alfredo Peña lived in splendid isolation. The lid of a tea chest served as a gate, and an array of sticks made up a fence, and his windows were shuttered with cardboard. Nobody respected Alfredo Peña's privacy: gangs of urchins rummaged and pilfered and spied, but Alfredo was oblivious to them all. He had drawn his parameters in the dust and he lived within its magic circle poring over the oily pages of his eclectic library.

At first, he had contested every page with the cockroaches that outnumbered and outflanked him. Then someone told him to soak all his books in kerosene, which he did, drying them laboriously and leaving a permanent chemical smell over his house, his clothes and himself. He thought of it as the incense of scholarship. What few belongings he'd had when he first arrived in the Barrio had long since been stolen. He didn't mind. The only things he valued were his tattered books, and since no one could read or write in the Barrio, nor had any desire to do so, and since no one knew anyone who could read or write, his books were as safe there as turds in a cesspit.

Alfredo had been examined and diagnosed by most of his neighbours and their unanimous verdict was that he was completely mad. There were two ways of looking at madmen in the Barrio, either you tormented them or you kept out of their way. All the efforts that had been made to tease him had proved in vain. It wasn't even that he didn't care: he didn't seem to notice. Nor was it imperative to keep out of the way of such a mild-mannered innocent. The Barrio was a collective of broken rules and broken lives held together by a new set of rules which the slum-dweller observed closely. Alfredo Peña ignored them all. Sometimes, his neighbours tried to fathom the alien depths of him, but since he seemed to live on a plain unknown to them, they gave up and then they ignored him. To say 'Good day' to Alfredo Peña was in itself a hazard. He was a purist, an interrogator of words and ideas.

'What do you mean by good? Is it really good in the sense that it is not an evil day? You can only perceive something that's good by a perception of something that's evil. They are mutually qualifying terms. Goodness can only exist by an awareness of evil. Take the fall from grace, for instance, have you ever wondered why . . .'

His monologues left his neighbours reeling. This didn't surprise him since thought always left him reeling too.

There were so many unresolved ideas in the world, and Alfredo Peña was shovelling like a lone miner in a mountain in search of seams of truth.

If Alfredo Peña had been a writer instead of a thinker, he could have written his biography in a few short paragraphs. The distraction which was to be the hallmark of his life started so early that he noticed very little of what had happened to him during his sixty years of research into the meaning of life. He'd been his mother's only child, but one of dozens of illegitimate sons of the local landowner. His mother was so ashamed of her bastard boy that she never asked the father to help support them; and her family were so ashamed of her that they turned her out. Society then cradled mother and child in such a way that should have ensured a miserable existence for both of them. They moved away and lived in tight-lipped penury. Alfredo was impervious to names, slights, and poverty, passing each day in a near trance, waiting for the night to come when he could continue his self-appointed task of counting the stars.

At fifteen, he discovered Ezra Pound. At sixteen, he discovered masturbation. At nineteen, he discovered T. S. Eliot. At twenty, his biological father discovered him and took him home to his great estate to live with him and his wife and learn the secrets of sugar cane farming. From a copy of the *Reader's Digest*, Alfredo first learnt of the astronomical theory of time. Time, as other people saw it, had never existed for Alfredo. He moved with a slowness of his own making. The surreal aspects of Alfredo's character proved too disturbing for his aged parent. In a family already swaddled through inbreeding with unacceptable layers of eccentricity, the sight of Alfredo's excessive calm drove the old man to apoplexy. Once his father died, the widow sent Alfredo packing, but not before he'd puzzled over the jigsaw of stars and how anyone could really know the distance to a given star. If you knew the speed at which light travels in a given year, and you measured the distance, but time itself is relative . . . So the deeper you look into space the more you look into the past. But how much more? And what is the past? Puzzling over this, and for no apparent reason, Alfredo had dismantled the American-built Squire cane crusher. He'd taken it to pieces: 138 pieces.

The widow swore never to let him set foot on her land again, but a year later, with the estate at a standstill and the giant cane crusher in a heap, she was reluctantly forced to send for him to see if, despite his apparent insanity, he could put it back together. It took him nine weeks, but he did it; and from that time, no one knew whether Alfredo Peña was a fool or a genius.

From being unemployable, he became in demand. Every sugar plantation in the state of Trujillo made use of, over the years, his one practical skill. From each house, he took part payment in books. There were, alas, few to choose from, yet each tome puzzled and muddled and fascinated him for months on end. The nuggets panned from these periods of intense study compounded as did the problems. The recurrence of these problems to his brain was as regular as the coming of the rains. And, like the rains, they silted up the side paths.

Life in the Barrio appeared at first glance to be a matter of formless squalor, yet it was constructed religiously around the five points of its star. These points were the places of pilgrimage to which the faithful inmates of the haphazard jungle at its centre made constant calls.

There was the road in, which was also the road out, with its traffic of runaways and refugees. Goods of all sorts were taken in, but no goods ever came out, with the exception of the funeral trappings which were hired out from the Church at Carmania and were rarely stolen. Otherwise, it was only people and garbage that came out of the Barrio. There were ladies of the night, a few girls in service in the town, petty criminals, boys on the razzle, drunks and endless mounds of litter that slipped down the hill. The people were all known to each other. Outsiders only came to the Barrio to look for trouble or to track down relatives who'd got into trouble. The Guardia Nacional never came at all, not even to conscript there; the Barrio policed itself, keeping its own laws and curfews. Gangs of boys set themselves up as vigilantes and guarded the road, sending strangers packing under showers of stones and broken glass. These boys weren't afraid of the Guardia Nacional, and they weren't afraid of fights, they were afraid of Alfredo Peña though: he talked nonsense and whispered spells. They despised his incantations and his dandruff, but they were not fooled by his mildness. Once, he had put a can of ginger biscuits outside his gate, with broken glass mixed in with them. He was sly.

On one side of the star-shaped Barrio, there was the rum shop where everyone went to drink or gossip or to carry home rum or ice or beer. Alfredo Peña never drank there and he never went there, not even for ice. The owner's wife hung a clove of garlic over her porch to keep away the spirits should he ever decide to call by. The owner's mistress, with her child's face perched incongruously on the grey voluptuous body of a sea cow, and her addiction to lime ice lollies which she consumed from noon till midnight, voiced what everyone thought. 'A man who doesn't drink isn't normal, isn't wholesome and probably isn't even Christian.' Beside her pile of discarded lolly sticks, she kept a crowbar, just in case the garlic didn't do the trick.

Then, next, there was the corrugated iron cabin where Cruz and her twin sister Magaly entertained men for free. Their house had to be made of iron, because anything else got burnt down by neighbours who earned an honest living plying their trade between the Barrio and Carmania. The only thing that was free in life was trouble, so what business had Cruz and Magaly to dole out pleasure for nothing and with such indefatigable zeal?

In the early years, there had been bad fights over it, but now that the sisters' charms had been battered beyond most men's desire, the legitimate trade suffered little loss, and the twins catered mostly for misfits, cripples and perverts, for which they were virtually forgiven their excessive generosity. Again, as though to flaunt his alien nature, Alfredo was the only male in the Barrio who hadn't held his nose at some time or another and been in for a tumble in the corrugated shack. If he wasn't a man, or even a pervert, what was he? The topic still came up for discussion in the rum shop as it did at the general store.

Alfredo Peña was not a popular customer at this store. He lived, so the owner claimed, on the borders of malnutrition. He never bought enough food to keep a guinea pig alive. A man who had owned not one, but over twenty cars and garaged them at the petrol station on the curve of the Panamericana like a visiting businessman, was obviously a tycoon. Tycoons were supposed to eat themselves into apoplexy, yet none of Alfredo's hidden fortune was really being spent at the store. He was mean. None of his hidden fortune was concealed in his house. That was common knowledge in the Barrio whose gangs of urchins took it in turns to ransack it. Meanness was all right when it went hand in hand with violence, but there was something disgusting about meanness on its own.

The last point of the Barrio's star was the shop that sold kerosene, candles and wicks. It was kept by El Turco Abran and his son. El Turco was not, as his name suggested, a Turk, but his powers of bargaining had earned him the title. For El Turco could haggle the back legs off a donkey and still make it carry its load. El Turco was also the Barrio's umpire, mediating between rival factions, blinding all comers with such a deluge of words that, although neither party could understand the half of them, both often went away satisfied to concoct some new quarrel. Of all the inhabitants of the Barrio, El Turco hated Alfredo Peña the most. He regarded Alfredo as a despicable fool while fearing his power to steal his own fire with his confounded rambling. El Turco regarded all words as his own personal property, to be loaned, at exorbitant rates of interest, to whoever paid him sufficient homage. He had been the undisputed champion of language until Alfredo came shuffling along, pretending to be half-witted so as to entangle his opponents. Such was his loathing of the man, that he had Alfredo's kerosene, candles and wicks delivered free of charge just to keep the rambling maniac out of his shop. Of course he overcharged him for his kerosene and had been doing so for twenty years, but it was a small revenge for the confusion Alfredo sowed in his territory. Alfredo was dangerous. He soaked his belongings in kerosene especially to mock El Turco Abran; he used it as an aftershave, carrying its odour with him everywhere like a goad.

Amid this mesh of fear, only Don Diego, who perhaps of anyone had studied Alfredo Peña the most, saw elements of saintliness in his subject. Don Diego was a stranger to the Barrio, but it was he who had given Alfredo his cars. He'd baled him out of his eight crashes and then finally persuaded him never to drive again. He felt an affection for Alfredo, yet his success with a cane crusher, no matter how complex, nor how many cogs and rollers it might have, was not reflected in his command of a motor car. He had tried both manual and automatic gears to no avail. The only person to be unperturbed by his accidents was Alfredo himself. He recalled not the smashes, or the carnage, the damage or the injuries to himself or others, he remembered only the quandaries that had induced them.

On the curve between Mendoza Fria and San Isidro, where the red and yellow petals of an acacia tree glittered through the mosaic leaves in the sun in a pattern as intricate as the illustrations of his *Guide to the Palace of the Alhambra*, Alfredo became lost in admiration for that distant treasure. Somewhere beyond Trujillo lay all the marvels of his books. He felt rich with their legacy. In his right hand, he held the cruelty and courage of Muley Abul Hassan and his treacherous son, Boabdil, in his left, he held the force of the Spanish monarchs who were to reconquer the beautiful palace. With his two hands thus engaged, he left the steering wheel unattended and his sky-blue Hillman free to meander into an irrigation ditch. No one knew how many hours later it was that Don Diego found him sitting in a patch of damp lilies with half his ribs broken and his shirt drenched in blood, but he was still pondering Muley Abul Hassan versus the Christian King and marvelling at the lattice works, mosaics and mocarabes of the Alhambra.

On the hill to Escuque, Alfredo Peña was struck by D. H. Lawrence's idea that the definition of genius is to be able to hold two completely conflicting ideas in one's head simultaneously and believe in both of them. He tested himself, and was thrilled to find it quite possible. He searched for words to describe the pleasure, failed and set aside the task and tried again: he needed two conflicting ideas and . . . He drove headlong into the kitchen of Aurelio Banderas, destroying the sanctity of his breakfast, his meagre furniture, his house, and the health of two of his six children.

In the market square of La Caldera, on market day, in front of hundreds of shoppers and Indian share-croppers down from the hills, Alfredo drove his Plymouth Valiant slowly but surely into a banana stand. Such was his concentration, that he stayed in the wreckage until he was dragged out by the irate crowd. What they took to be concussion was actually one of Alfredo's regular trances as he recited Eliot to himself in Spanish:

> *Time present and time past*
> *Are both perhaps present in time future*
> *And time future contained in time past.*
> *If all time is eternally present*
> *All time is unredeemable.*

Alfredo Peña moved through his life at a snail's pace. Nothing had ever hurried him and it seemed that nothing could. He drove at a speed well under twenty miles an hour. Other cars often crashed into him out of sheer exasperation, so his vehicles were always alarmingly battered, with bits of mudguard, mirrors and doors clattering along behind him. If one were to count all these knocks, the tally of his accidents would run into three figures. Don Diego counted only the occasions when bones were broken or blood was drawn. Alfredo rarely emerged from his abstraction sufficiently to find the reverse gear, but since when he did, he often stayed there, wheeling backwards into whatever oncoming traffic happened to be tackling the roads that day, Alfredo's saintly qualities were ignored on the highways, and he came to be considered a menace.

At night, by the light of his kerosene lamp, with the heavy scent of jasmine laced with kerosene in the air, Alfredo whispered Eliot to himself:

> *Because these wings are no longer wings to fly*
> *But merely vans to beat the air*
> *The air which is now thoroughly small and dry*
> *Smaller and dryer than the will*
> *Teach us to care and not to care*
> *Teach us to sit still.*

The clamour of the Barrio filled the tropical sky with screams and moans, shrieks and laughter that dulled to little more than the background throb of cicadas and tree frogs battering the darkness. Alfredo had a habit of twisting his naturally silky curls around his fingers and pulling at them as though his true understanding of any given line had somehow adhered to his hair.

Don Diego, who was one of the few literate members of his society, spent many interesting hours in the company of Alfredo Peña, discussing Plato, Thomas Mann, Tolstoy, Eliot and Pound with him. Whenever he had time on his hands, it was refreshing to ramble through books in that cultural backwater. They lived in Philistine times. It was almost more extraordinary than Alfredo's learning that he had managed to find any books at all: like corsets and swords, they belonged to a lost generation. Don Diego himself was considered an intellectual simply because he drove into town sometimes and perused the newspaper. He would have dearly liked to expose Alfredo to more sources, but the available texts were limited. Don Diego, who had twice travelled to the capital in his youth, had seen such miracles of scholarship as bookshops and public libraries. Sometimes, though, it was as hard to describe such places to Alfredo as it was to describe the sea to his plantation workers. Eventually, he realised that Alfredo could not have coped with such quantities of thoughts, his pace was not designed for the scholarly avalanche. His selection of literary pickings, his slim volumes suited him. He enjoyed measuring out his learning in coffee spoons, preferring to tap one vein than to follow the myriad other ones.

Once, as they sat sipping fresh cane juice under the shade of a guava tree, whiling away the dead hours of the afternoon, Don Diego had suggested that since Alfredo so enjoyed certain poems, by T. S. Eliot in particular, he should learn some English so as to read them in the original. Alfredo was speechless with surprise and dismay. He revered Don Diego (as much as he was capable of revering anyone outside the covers of a book) and it astonished him that his friend could be so stupid. Why go to all the trouble of memorising some incomprehensible gibberish when it was already perfectly clearly written in one's own tongue? Alfredo knew what he was talking about – he had seen a newspaper printed in a foreign script, and he had heard Mr

Lee (the Chinaman from Trinidad who spoke English to his canaries and lived in town) speak in his native language. From the time of Don Diego's suggestion, Alfredo Peña looked on his friend and patron with suspicion tinged by regret. No matter what arguments Don Diego used, Alfredo clung to his belief in Cristiano (as he called Spanish). For him, there was only one valid language, and he had learnt it at his mother's knee.

Though it was true that when he drove Don Diego's new Ford into the side of the Mototán bus it was through dwelling on this problem of other languages. It was not, as he insisted later from his hospital bed, because he believed for an instant in the need to trouble his already troubled brain with foreign vocabularies, but because it had occurred to Don Diego that he might want to do so. Why! He had the books themselves at home in the Barrio! They were stacked on Pepsi tins to protect them from the floods. Don Diego could go and verify, in fact he must do so. Hardy, Eliot, Pound, Plato and Baudelaire: strange names indeed; but all clearly written in Cristiano. The evidence was there, in print, in his own room.

Don Diego, who would have rather walked naked into his own cane factory furnace than set foot in the notorious Barrio, had to promise he would go and see for himself. Nothing else would convince Alfredo in his sick bed, and since the patient was tearing perilously at his tubes and drips, he assured him that he would go. Sometimes, it was best to humour Alfredo, which was, after all, what everyone else had been doing for years.

On the last day of Alfredo's life, he had been mounting a new cane crusher for Don Diego. He had been mounting it for fourteen months, achieving so little each week that his patron had at last begun to understand the apoplexy of Alfredo's father. Their own discussions had all but ceased; Alfredo's mind had slowed to such an aggravating degree that conversation, even for them, was virtually impossible. Every word and every hair was split. Don Diego had begun to choose his questions carefully, hoping to avoid hours of philosophy in response to his every comment. Perhaps it was the heat wave, but Don Diego no longer found Alfredo's calm either beatific or amusing.

Lunch that day had been an interminable affair. Alfredo had said, not once, but thrice, 'Have you ever noticed how . . .?'

By two o'clock, it was clear that Alfredo would not be doing another stroke of work. Not so much as a screw or bolt would be added to the great unfinished machine. The fact that Alfredo had summoned Don Diego from his uneasy siesta out into the sweltering sun to witness his idleness, galled him. Worse still, he knew that he would be in for a slow haul across Hegel. For the past five weeks, Alfredo had traced his way across the ideas of the German philosopher. 'We stand in a momentous time, a seething mass, in which the mind has made a sudden bound, left its old shape behind and is gaining a new. The whole bulk of our old ideas, the very bands of the world, are rent asunder, and collapse like a dream . . .'

Don Diego's liver was giving him hell. He had once

(and only once) mentioned this to Alfredo, and the subsequent verbal circumnavigation of hell had lasted for two months.

Alfredo was at full tilt, his battered panama hat was rammed firmly over his grey hair, his face was radiant with enlightened thought, and his mouth was shaping slowly into an 'I wonder why . . .?' Don Diego felt himself shiver as though someone had walked over his grave. The words would drag out in that slow monotone, and he hadn't the heart to hear Alfredo's scratched disc again.

'Come on,' he said, 'I'll drive you back.'

'Backwards or forwards, now I wonder why we say . . .' Alfredo twiddled his dwindling curls.

'Get in!' Diego insisted, opening the passenger door of his pick-up truck while suppressing the urge to pull Alfredo's hair.

Alfredo sat silently mouthing as they jolted away from the sugar mill to the bridge and then up the rough track to the road. The road, as Don Diego had often explained proudly, had been built through the estate when his father was Governor, enabling them to take their sugar straight out from the dirt track on to the Panamerican Highway. The only disadvantage was that the slope up to it rendered access blind. Don Diego always told his drivers never to drive straight out without stopping. You had to lean out and look, or ask the passenger to. The halt was second nature to him.

By the time he reached the tarmac lip and braked, Don Diego felt sorry for his anger. Alfredo was all right really and he was immune to both rage and reproach. Don Diego watched him mouthing still, 'The very bands of the world are rent asunder, and collapse like a dream.'

'Alfredo, is there a car coming?'

Alfredo leant out slowly and looked carefully to the left and to the right. 'No,' he said, drawing out his words and reaching for a grey curl, as Don Diego accelerated left, 'there isn't a car . . . there's a . . . lorry!'

Zapa, the fire child who looked like a toad

On the east side of the hacienda, on the slope that stretched across from the rift of hidden orange trees to the low crest, La Ciega's house spread down the hill in a series of low-roofed mud walls that lengthened and expanded with his family. La Ciega was both rich and blind. He had been so for many years. He was an optimist, so he never accepted his lack of sight. The fortune that he was amassing from his illicit still and his continual sales of rot-gut rum would, he believed, one day pay for the miracle that would return his sight to him. Because La Ciega was also a realist, he knew that even miracles had to be paid for; only calamity was free. So he kept his money in a pit under the hearth like a hoard of future visions. Since he didn't care for his money as such, what he wanted was to see, he never felt that just his savings made him rich. His true riches lay in the cropped heads of his many sons and in the thick hair of his daughters. La Ciega had fifteen children: fourteen of his own and his orphaned niece, the fire child Zapa.

When the rains turned all the tracks to mud and hindered the working of the old copper distillery and leaked through the tin roofs, blackened the corncakes and mildewed the pots, all the workers used to find their way to La Ciega's to drink there and describe his children to him. Elsa, his favourite, was the prettiest with her hair like a fair horse's mane and eyes the colour of smothered grass. The plainest – not only of his, but of all the estate children – was Zapa, who never had a proper name. Somehow, though he did favour Elsa, the blind man loved these two girls nearly the same. Had not Zapa been given to him, and she was his kin, saved as a baby from a burning hut; people called her survival a miracle. La Ciega loved miracles, even if they happened to other people. They inspired him rather in the way his own gold teeth inspired the workers. Few men were envious of his gold-studded mouth; there was a collective pride in his metal dentistry. It was enough just to live near such a mouth: to sit and speak and hear the answers tumbling from the shrinking barricades.

Zapa was so plain that it had given her her name. It meant 'a toad'. When she was first dragged from the fire, saved by her screams (and the natural curiosity that always lured the workers and their families to the site of a disaster), she was only a few weeks old. At first they thought that Zapa's mother was in the hut as well and that they'd watched her burn. But when the ashes cooled and the debris was checked, there was no sign of any bones except for the charred splinters of the guinea pigs trapped in their inner pen. For weeks and months they thought her mother would return to claim her baby, but she never came. Waiting for her, they felt reluctant to choose a name, so they called her Zapa to match her strange face, and the nickname stuck to her, as she to them.

No one knew what made her perform her odd rituals; only Elsa seemed to understand the importance of crouching on stones and staring silently into water. Every day Elsa and Zapa shared their chores, sweeping the dirt floors and making brooms, gathering twigs for kindling and grinding corn; then all their spare time would be spent inventing games, making shrines and saying chants into the dark rift of trees. Zapa was always the high priestess, while Elsa, who was four years older, was the acolyte.

Every year, when the rains stopped and the layer of mould that had gathered on everything – from the hammock strings to the used milk tins that sat clustered around their house, with their muddy geraniums – had powdered and dried, people began to gossip again. It was not that they stopped during the rainy season, it was just that the floods, and the inevitable sickness and fever that followed, held back the tide of conjecture. There was less time for speculation. The workers still monitored each other's affairs, but they laid down their stores of information like salt fish for such time as they might need them. Life took longer to live in the wet weather. The best place to gossip was on the low wall outside La Ciega's and the track was too slippery then, and the wall itself too chilly.

La Ciega was a money-lender – not by any special inclination, more because he was the only person other than the *patron* who had any money. Everyone, in their time, would wind up the steep slope to his house and borrow from him, watching him notch the tally on to his lending stick. Then, within minutes, everyone else for miles around would know about the transaction. There were no secrets on the hacienda. Nothing was or could be hidden except for the tops of the tall orange trees that grew in the dank rift of the valley. In lieu of interest, La Ciega charged information. Blind as he was, he made himself the centre of that world. Nothing moved without his knowledge. No wedding or funeral was possible without his loans. No bribe or debt could be paid without his assistance. Because instead of drudging in the cane fields he had the wit to distil the cane juice, he was treated somewhat as an oracle. Any man who could prosper despite his disability, have fifteen children all clothed and fed, a gold mouth, and an unlimited stash of inside information must be wiser than most, without a doubt. So when the wives and the widows sent their children across the pink tasselled grass to fill up their empty bottles with new rum, or to borrow the coins for a new sack of seed, they often asked Ciega for his advice on this or that dispute.

To his own household, he said: 'I am like the old man of Mototán. My voice is the voice of all this valley. They live their lives by mine, just as we all live ours by the sun's clock. Their sons and daughters fear me because I have my fingers caught in all their parents' veins. In the beginning all I wanted was to see, but now, though I am blind, I can see that the example I lease to others must come from me.'

La Ciega's wife had heard this speech before and she would sidle back into her kitchen before he got halfway through, smiling with a mixture of pride and mockery. Perhaps because she never had to borrow money from him, she didn't find him as imposing as the others. Or perhaps it was because he was helpless without her and she had borne him fourteen children. When the elections came round, filling the towns and villages with their bribes, La Ciega and his wife, Juana, had been to hear some of the speeches. Maybe Juana smiled at her husband because she recognised the rhetoric as coming from the Christian Democrat campaigner who had given them the new copper pipes for their stills. Whatever the reason, Juana never showed the others her ambiguous smile. It was something she kept for herself as she patted out the corncakes for their evening meal.

It was only the words that came between them, because Juana, too, wanted her sons home by nightfall. It kept her from worrying, and it kept them safe. She knew herself how easily led astray a girl could be – even by a blind man. Her family had once teased her for her marriage. She supposed they must have despised La Ciega. In principle she did too, but in practice he was too fine a man to harbour any prejudice against. And who else had a husband with a headful of gold? And who else had as many live children, or seen half as much food? So Juana was happy with her lot, and as watchful as her husband for her children's safety. There was no shame in her family, no blot, and it was a fine thing to be envied by so many other women. Not even their gossiping scratches reached their mark. What did it matter that La Ciega had never been able to see her fine looks? He had felt her and loved her, and now that child-birth had harrowed her flesh, she was glad that he would never see her face fade. She saw her beauty repeated in Elsa with pride, and she saw the poor thin hair and the pale wide mouth of her niece with pity. Poor Zapa; La Ciega loved her because she was his sister's child, his blood. But Juana loved her for her motherlessness. Her own daughters were so pretty that Zapa's lack of grace never bothered her; she was a good girl, and that was all that mattered.

Zapa rarely paused to think about her place in the family; she was neither the eldest nor the youngest. Her chores were simple and her rewards were greater than the dusty mugs of syrupy water for the poor children on the estate. On Sunday she ate eggs and chicken and sardines with her rice. She had a comb of her own, and a new cotton frock every Christmas time, and sandals for her feet. Sometimes she thought of her real mother, the one who had left her to burn, but she could never put a face to the idea. When the sun was at its hottest, and the yard and rooms were swept and the brooms had been dismantled and fresh twigs had been collected for the afternoon's sweep, Zapa would lie in the grass and squint at the sun, searching for a hint of her lost mother. The lights in front of her eyelids were as near as she ever came to seeing her, red and orange lights that hovered on the edge of sleep.

Most days, though, she was content with her passport to love, and her cult of the swept yard and her games and Elsa. She knew that everyone needed to belong somewhere, and she did, right there on her uncle's porch every night at six when the silent curfew filled the hills and all the weary workers staggered back home across the terraces. The drag-bellied pigs were shut away for the night, as were the hens and goats. La Ciega's lumpy cow was tethered and his dogs unleashed. All the stray children divided and scattered to their own places to eat and rest. Everyone was counted. Not even the boys missed the beginning of the curfew. It was true that they crept out again sometimes, but the world as they knew it began and ended at six and six. An enor-mous amount of scandal could be squeezed in between those times, but the times themselves were sacred. Work began and ended then. It seemed, almost, as though life itself began and ended there too.

For eight years Zapa had learned to ply her broom, then for two years she was mistress of the sweeping. She mastered her craft so well that she knew all the places where the escoba bush grew, and she picked the twigs faster and tied them quicker than any other child. Sometimes people would come and ask to borrow her so that she might make up their brooms. Zapa could make brooms that would last a whole week. She had a knack of stuffing the bundle of twigs through the cut cylinder of an empty sardine tin in such a way that the twigs would stay put. People used to poke at her straggly hair and say, 'Juana did a good job the day she dragged you screaming from that fire. And to think all we saw was a bundle of rags and burns, when really you were an infant prodigy. What do you say to that, Zapa?'

But Zapa was a shy child who had, some said, lost her tongue in the fire. Often, instead of answering, she would hold up the backs of her hands and flash her fingernails. It was her way of communicating. Only Elsa knew how much she loved to chatter. When there were just the two of them playing in the rift, Zapa never stopped talking. She'd squat on her favourite flat stone and blink her wide eyes and make up reasons for everything around them. Zapa could explain the existence of every seed and fruit; she'd pretend to know how the sand and the boulders came to be there. She would watch the blue birds settling in the tree tops and then tell Elsa where they came from and where they were going to. Zapa could trace the tracks of the red ants and list the nests of the beetles and lizards who clung to the rocks. Whatever Elsa asked her, Zapa knew. She seemed to take the cobwebs that looped from one wide leaf of the red-studded onoto to the next and weave them into gossamer lies. She told Elsa that God had given her the face of a toad so that everyone would notice only her beautiful hands.

'Look,' she'd say, showing her manicured fingers yet again. 'Look, not even the *doña* has hands like mine. I could sweep the porch down to its bare bone and my skin would still be as soft and my nails as fine.'

Elsa loved Zapa's hands. She worshipped them and begged her to tell the secrets of the potions and leaves that she rubbed into them. Sometimes Zapa shared her spells, mixing up creams for Elsa, but she never told her how they were made. When the first signs of the workers' return

56

home drifted up to them, they would make their way home. Zapa often lingered for a while in the wood, but she never missed the curfew – no one did. No one dared.

The day had begun like any day. It was not special, there was no saint hovering over it. There was no market out of range or visitor on the estate. Elsa had seen Antonio José, her admirer, but then she saw him every day. He wanted to marry her but she was only fourteen and he didn't seem like half as much fun as staying at home, where there was plenty of everything, and sleeping near Zapa, whom she loved. Zapa was only ten and would have years to go until she married, so Antonio José would have to wait or choose again. After the sweeping, she and Zapa had gone to the rift. Their frangipangi tree had opened its first flower, and Zapa had caught a frog and a water snake in her net. Elsa had wanted to tie the frog in a plantain bag and then watch it struggle, but Zapa had told her that this frog was the keeper of all the flowers, and a special friend of hers who came in through the hole in the kitchen door; if they let it be, it would sing 'Las Mañanitas' to them next year. Then Elsa went home and Zapa said she'd follow.

It had been a day of little things with nothing but a trickle of trivia to show for itself. Nothing had happened to announce its importance. There were no portents, no kneeling boughs or tapping winds, no formation of birds in flight. Nothing. In years to come, Elsa felt retrospectively cheated by this. She looked back and sifted the events, the whispers and comments, searching for some significance or some pattern to explain why their lives were shattered then. But there was nothing.

Elsa sat on the porch and waited impatiently. It never occurred to her that Zapa would be really late. No one was ever late. She waited uneasily only because the quality of her own life improved when Zapa was beside her. The others began to grumble long before she began to feel alarm. Zapa had a reason and an excuse for everything; she would find a way to darn her absence to the law. If only she came back and she could make La Ciega forgive her, but she didn't come. Juana began to move in slow motion, the paste of wet corn started to stick to her fingers. In retrospect, she would call this the first omen. As the moments passed, the thin house filled with dread. The boys tried to laugh off the tension; but one by one they found themselves swallowing teazles as La Ciega ran through and repeated his head count.

At dawn and dusk, the double six of every day, each child knelt before La Ciega and his tally stick. The blind man would reach out and touch each proffered crown.

'Bless me, father.'

'May god bless you and your life be good.'

Fourteen varying heads passed under his palm. He knew them all so well.

'Where is Zapa?' he asked each time, running and rerunning the head count through his hands.

'Where is Zapa?'

La Ciega had a gold fob watch which he kept on a chain round his neck for safekeeping. Between each demand he called out, 'Pedro – time?'

It was six fifteen, eighteen, twenty-three, six thirty, then seven o'clock and eight. Elsa watched, taking her ritual part in the charade, passing and repassing in her place in the count. She watched Zapa's prospective scolding turned into a beating and then a thrashing, and then take off into the realms of the unknown. She was tempted to run and find her, but she knew that such action would be a clumsy admission of a guilt that Elsa felt sure Zapa would be able to explain away.

The night was thick with shadows when Zapa walked up to the line of stunned silence. Her family all looked to her to ease their confusion and the chill that was coming from the evening air into the base of their spines. Elsa watched her adoptive sister's wispy hair caught in the small light of their lamp. She remembered there were fireflies in the bracken and trees around her. As though by Zapa's orchestration, the cicadas began to sing with their usual tunelessness as she arrived. All she had to do was to speak up over their low background of noise, and Zapa was always good with insects.

The minutes of waiting became worse than the preceding two hours. Zapa said nothing except, kneeling, she asked for her '*Bendicion*'.

Their world fragmented in La Ciega's silence. The blessing was refused: the house was shamed, and Zapa herself condemned, with never so much as a word spoken.

The others pushed and poked her and made eyes such as could roll excuses from behind their own sockets. Zapa said nothing except for the three times she knelt in front of her uncle and asked for his blessing. By the third denial, Juana had Zapa's bundle ready for her: the frock and comb, her emery boards and a stack of corncakes for the night. She handed it to the child to make her see how final her silence would be. Zapa took it sadly, looking around her with her wide, slightly protruding eyes.

'*Bendicion*?' she asked, this time of Juana. In reply there were only that tired woman's tears, which seemed to speak more clearly than any words might have done: 'May He forgive, Zapa, for you know we can't. You have brought shame into this house, you must take it away again.' Zapa took the bundle and shuffled backwards across the porch, avoiding Elsa's eyes. She held out her hand to Juana, who had been a mother: '*Bendicion*, Mamma?'

No one ever knew why Zapa wouldn't explain where she had been, not even Elsa. It couldn't have changed everything, whatever the excuse, but the leaving would have been more gentle had words been allowed to bear witness. As it was, Zapa found herself making her way through the dark, past the barking dogs of every hut that lay between home and the road that she would have to reach to leave the hacienda. There was nowhere else to go but away. No one would dare to go against La Ciega. Zapa knew that no one would want to. Men and women who had turned their own daughters away for just such misdemeanours would scarcely harbour her, after what she had done. She had broken the form, and the form was everything. She had splintered their life. The lust that she was tacitly accused of had no reason to escape at such a time. Dozens of bastards were conceived in the night between the blessings. By defying La Ciega she had made herself a rebel woman in the eyes of the world and shunned his protection.

As she picked her way over the loose stones of the track, the implications of her loss began to possess her. She walked past the low-slung avocado trees and the leaves rustled against her face. There were noises all around her, the night noises that she had been brought up to fear. Anyone who went out at night was prey to El Coco, the wild man who ate children like herself. Only a lover and a great deal of lust could conquer such fears. Zapa had neither. Juana would assume that Zapa had been led astray by a man – were it not so, she would have talked in her defence and mitigated her sentence to being banished into service. Zapa didn't know why she hadn't talked. Even without her usual weave of fantasy she could have told the truth: she had fallen asleep on a huge cold stone. The fire took her tongue.

It didn't take long to flush Zapa out from the dusty roadside to the town. A few days spent hanging around the market scrounging for food soon brought her down to the place where she would be cared for. It even seemed vaguely like a mythical home. She was taken to the Calle Vargas, a street of brothels on the far side of the little market town. She had never seen or heard of the red-light zone before, but she liked the sound of it. It was all she felt of her mother, that flicker of red lights on her eyelids when the sun beat down.

The women on the Vargas were mostly kind, but the turnover was fast, so no one really had time to help a ten-year-old child prostitute with an ugly face and a broad grin, wide eyes and a lack of grace.

Some of the old regulars who had proved themselves immune to the fevers and the infections remembered her. They remembered her plainness and her impossibly thin hair and her gift for sweeping and her perfect nails. She had won several hearts by doing the manicures in between customers. 'Poor Zapa,' they would say, 'she had some very nasty customers.'

When Elsa married Antonio José, she did so to gain her freedom to seek Zapa out. As a married woman, she had the right to go to market. She hadn't wanted to wed so young, but somewhere she knew that Zapa needed her, and life itself was empty without Zapa. She didn't love Antonio José, but she preferred him to her life at Ciega's house as it had come to be since Zapa left. Everyone missed her. After Elsa's marriage a whole year passed before she tracked her sister down. It was a year of buying herbs and asking questions. By then, it was nearly three years since Zapa had gone. It was possible for Elsa to get to market only occasionally. She didn't know what would happen when she found Zapa; just that she had to look.

Elsa followed Zapa as she shifted from one brothel to the next, never quite managing to catch up with her in the minutes she stole from her shopping trips. Elsa left notes and messages and presents of soft cheese and eggs. At one point she seemed so close, but when she returned, they said Zapa had fled.

One by one her own babies were born, weighing her down as they filled her womb and tying her down at home. She had less time to search for her sister. Whenever she did, the news was confusing. Zapa had gone, disappeared, died of a fever, died of a fight, run away with a cowboy, run away with a gambler, found her family, gone home. Eventually Elsa despaired, and made a shrine to Zapa in the rift, loading it with flowers and leaves and piles of flat grey stones. Every time she felt her breasts harden and a new life stir within her, she prayed tearfully for the sign of a toad in her womb.

The bolshybally

I t pleased La Rusa to surround herself with mystery. She had furnished her sitting room with it, knotting the drapes in such a way that the twisted folds seemed to conceal secrets that La Rusa wasn't telling. It was rumoured that the hollow ring that gave the style its bulk when she had finished pinning and poking her thin chestnut hair into place was filled with gold and diamonds. No one had ever been close enough to her to rummage through her hair, though mealtimes all over the town were spent discussing where the Russian lady kept her hoard, and where she came from. The general consensus of opinion was that she was not Russian at all. Yet, despite twenty years of interest in her origins and her affairs, no one had managed to bring up any conclusive proof against her.

Judge Gomez swore that he had known La Rusa carnally in a whore-house in Bogotá many years before. But Judge Gomez had been known to mistake his own daughter for the old laundress who pressed his wife's linen, so his evidence had to be dismissed as unreliable. Word had it that La Rusa came from a backstreet of Maracay. She was also said to have grown up in a corrugated shack by the curves of

San Pedro on the desert road that led to Barquisimeto. A German girl who worked shifts for La Rusa claimed that the boss was a German from the Colony Tovar. Whatever the truth might be about La Rusa's nationality, it was clear that she herself was never going to enlighten either her clients or her girls. She spoke a smattering of French, and she cursed in an unrecognisable language. There was a photograph of the late Tsar and Tsarina over the grand piano in her room, together with a page from a magazine with a picture of the grand Duchess Anastasia.

In her youth, La Rusa had liked to let slip hints and remarks about the missing Anastasia, as though to imply that by some miracle she had been resurrected to run an elegant brothel in the Andes. She had seen the film at least a dozen times, and she had adopted a number of mannerisms from the screen, together with a soft throaty way of rolling her rrr's. For years it had thrilled her to be taken for the royal refugee, and she would have continued to fantasise had not some interfering pedant worked out the ages and asked her point blank if she could really be nearing sixty. If only they knew, all those people struggling on their ant hill of a town, how much she did have in common with the famous Anastasia. For she too had the whole world against her, needling to uncover her identity; and she was friendless, despite her wealth and her position as empress of the red-light zone. Each of her girls had more friends than she. Sometimes it seemed that she was doomed to be a female Judas of prostitution, predestined to take the silver and be shunned. Sometimes she felt quite sad and bitter about her lot, but not so bitter that a drop of rum mixed with lemon and honey could not ease the thoughts away. The sun would work its way around her yard with tyrannical indifference every day. The mornings would begin to throb with the gathering heat, and flies and mosquitoes would try to squeeze through the protective mesh that veiled every window of the house. The afternoons would swelter, slowly unravelling the tapestry of her life. It was hard to be elegant in such heat. The silk around her body crumpled and her hair mutinied in sticky wisps. The afternoons were a time for vigilance, the sentry duty that led up to the ritual opening of her court. At half-past six sharp the painted carousel that gave La Rusa's 'Rainbow' so much of its character began to run, rising and falling to the hurdy gurdy underneath its maypole centre. Side-saddle on each multicoloured horse sat one of her girls.

It was a privilege to work for La Rusa. The money was good and the prestige was important. Anyone who had sat for more than six months on the carousel at the Rainbow could be sure to find another job anywhere within a radius of 200 miles. And it was a fact that it was easier to marry out of La Rusa's than it was to marry off the street. It was true, too, that no one really knew her, or particularly liked her, but she showed no weaknesses and therefore gave no hold for anyone to understand or care for her as a person. Hundreds of girls were grateful to her for giving them the social education that would otherwise always have remained out of their reach. La Rusa might have been a leading lady in many of the not-so-local weddings where girls from the

Rainbow married into respectable families; yet the very nature of her business excluded her from such social gatherings. She would have given the game away to the other side. Her own secrets were enclosed in a kernel in the centre of a nut of other secrets. La Rusa was not just a famous madam, she was also an enigma.

She ruled her world without any potions or visible spells. While her girls spent their free afternoons roaming through the covered market looking for persuasive roots and herbs, La Rusa would stay at home playing one of the three tunes she knew on her tarnished piano. Although the entire neighbourhood was sick of these hammered tunes, La Rusa never was. On the days when her self-administered tots of honeyed rum were most generous, she would arrange herself in a certain position on the faded gold brocade of her *chaise-longue*, and summon one of her minions to her as though she were the grande dame of Hollywood she felt she might have been, had circumstances been otherwise. Her girls came to her by rota, carrying an old-fashioned usherette's tray laden with emery boards and oils. Then, while her nails were manicured, La Rusa would tell of her night of glory.

She liked the prettiest girls best. She liked them to kneel at her feet while she unwrapped her story. There were always girls who wanted to get close to her, either to share her business or to steal it. There were girls who were bribed by clients to discover her secrets. Within the hierarchy of the Rainbow it would have been worth a lot to have been La Rusa's confidante. There was power and security in her friendship. But no one ever managed to become her friend. They were all called in, in their turn, to her festooned chamber on the ground floor, yet the web that she spun was too frail for any of them to grasp and her gossamer was wasted. She listened to the mixture of relief and mockery that followed each manicurist out of her silken trap. There was usually a huddle of girls waiting on the galleried landing.

'What did she tell you? What did she say?'

'Just the bolshybally.'

The ripples of laughter drifted down to her backstate door.

'Not again! Didn't you ask her about the matinée?'

'Why didn't you ask her something new?'

The day's manicurist would put her tray away in the small cupboard at the top of the stairs and say, 'So what's new? You know she's got bally on the brain. She just keeps you away with it.'

Back in one of their tightly shuttered bedrooms the girls held an emergency meeting. Behind La Rusa's back, they decided their every action at these summits, pooling their thoughts so as to undermine her own.

It was a small room with a mosaic tiled floor and white-washed walls. In one corner there stood an iron-frame washbowl and jug and a large bar of soap. In another corner there was a small plaster of Paris madonna propped against a crudely painted black-faced Saint Benito. Both of them were peeling from the heat of the fat votive candle that flickered at their feet. Beneath a plastic crucifix, the metal bed bulged and rippled under puce satin flounces chequered with sombre linen embroidery squares that were herring-boned on to its slippery surface. La Rusa encouraged the girls to do needlework during the dead hours of the afternoon. She said it calmed them down while training them in a ladylike skill. It was, at least, a useful way for the girls to cover up the unsavoury stains that were part and parcel of their profession. Some of the girls were nearly forty now, had worked for La Rusa for the best part of their lives. One or two of them were on their second layer of linen squares, and had long since passed the marriageable age. They were desperate to share in La Rusa's secrets and profits before old age robbed them of their work. Of these such girls, Angelica with her dark brown eyes and thick, ready fists was the leader.

'Listen, I worked in a lot of places before I came here, and I tell you it is not natural. You can't have a madam and no favourite. You just can't have that; it isn't right. La Rusa has told me that she doesn't care for me or any one of us more than another. And that is not right. She calls it fair. Well life isn't fair. And when things aren't natural then they're not safe either. That old bitch is killing this town with curiosity.'

'Angelica, what's the matter with that? It's too hot to get bothered. We get our money, we're happy here and I bet we do get to see the matinée, too.'

'For the love of God, can't you see we're in danger? What will happen here if La Rusa runs out to her bolshy-bally? She's capable of it, she goes on about it enough: "If I could have leapt as I saw them leap that night I would never have been a whore. I would have leapt, Angelica, leapt through the air like time itself in suspension . . ." So, girls, what happens here if the old bat disappears?'

Sofia, the girl who had answered before, spoke again, curling her legs up under her with a languorous slither that seemed to imply that any movement at all was an effort too great for her pale pampered limbs. 'If La Rusa bales out, Angelica, you can run the show together with a junta, and we'll all make heaps of money; but bags I don't have to do any more work.'

Maria Eugenia, who had joined the Rainbow during the rainy season and so was the newest of them all, had a habit of watching everyone with an air of wounded innocence which made her very popular with the older clients. She was watching now, turning her tawny wide-open eyes from one speaker to the next. 'I agree with Angelica. We do the work here. They all use us, but they come for La Rusa. She's the main attraction. Trade would fall off, you'd see, if it weren't for her and her bally secrets.'

'What's so urgent about now, though. What's new?'

'She's getting restless, that's what. She's lonely. She's calling us down more. Her fingernails are nearly worn away.'

Downstairs a giant insect began to buzz and shake and hum before settling into the rhythmic beating of the generator.

'Good God, it's nearly time to start; quick, get dressed, and get the rooms cleared.'

Downstairs, La Rusa was marking time with her fingertips on the carved back of her throne. This half hour before

73

opening was her favourite time. From the corner of her eye she saw a mosquito caught in a new spider's web, and she sighed. There was intrigue in the air again. There would be another attempt, no doubt, at a palace revolution soon. It was silly for the girls to try. Surely they knew that she had more to her than they, she had survived the cold winds of the Steppes and wolves, wild Tartars and Cossacks' swords. She had held on to life by its claws through war and famine. She too had lain injured under trucks of straw and been smuggled through the plains. Well, Angelica knew, but maybe the others didn't, because she didn't talk about that part of her life so much any more; not since they'd started selling the *Great Book of Facts* from door to door in the town and some of her details had become blurred, it seemed. It was such a long time ago. She was a mere child then. It was even before she saw the ballet and discovered the secret of life.

The organ would begin to play soon, tantalising the men in the streets. In the time waiting for the curtain to rise and the show to begin she could imagine herself in another place waiting to see another stage. Or maybe tonight would be the night the girls and the music made that magic in her brain. It had happened before, only once before, on the night of the Bolshoi Ballet.

The spider's web

L_a Rusa was spending her second year in bed, and her fantasies were running dry. Although she was still, nominally, the Madame of the finest brothel in the neighbourhood, her life at the Rainbow was more like that of a spider trapped in her own web. In another month the rainy season would begin. And another month would see the anniversary of the time when she fell down the stairs and broke her back. Every morning, as her girls slept and only the sound of insects relieved the monotony of the silence, La Rusa tried not to feel again the push that had sent her down the carved staircase. Falls were healthier. Pushes had too many other implications. She was a helpless invalid; it didn't do to dwell on how she came to be so.

Beyond the slatted shutters and the grid iron bars, across the street, lay Maria Elena Rosales who had been shrivelling back to a sackful of bones and skin for the last ten years. She was wasting away without a murmur of complaint. Some of the girls, fascinated by the illness that had taken on aspects of a magician's act, monitored her gradual disappearance and declared her a saint. The same could never be said for La Rusa whose only relief from the fear and humiliation of her condition was to protest in an out-raged monologue that continued in whispers, even in her sleep. It could have been guilt or merely boredom that kept the girls away from the icon-filled relic of La Rusa's room, but for whatever reason, she spent most of her hot helpless hours on her own.

Nobody knew for sure how the new girl came to be sit-ting on the end of La Rusa's bed that day when the morning coffee was brought. The other girls went down and scrutinised the intruder. They themselves all ranged in age between fifteen and forty (although the older ones would not admit this much) while the new girl, as La Rusa called her, was no bigger than a child of seven. She was also excessively pale, and wide-mouthed, with an unnatural pallor that made her look like a flat-faced toad. Her round freckled eyes were disturbingly knowing in their expression.

'This child has come to sit with me in my solitude,' La Rusa announced. When the girls had left her, she turned to the newcomer, and laughed for the first time since her accident.

'What will they make of that?' she gloated. 'What will they think?'

They thought it was witchcraft, and upstairs, all the old potions and spells were brought out of their drawers and boxes. Ilario Gomez, who took the money and paid the wages and the bills in La Rusa's stead now that she was unable to hold her own purse strings anymore, declared that the new girl had crawled through the window bars, drawn in by La Rusa's incessant muttering.

La Rusa herself had no doubt in her mind that this child companion had arrived by means of a miracle. She would have liked to have woven her arrival into the story of the lost grand duchess: to make the waif an emissary from the doomed court of Russia. But since the child refused to speak about herself, and had a dazed, almost half-witted air about her, it seemed best just to tell her about the Russian royal family rather than try to turn her into one of them. The mystery of La Rusa's own origins no longer kept the townspeople debating into the night. Nobody seemed to care anymore whether she was or was not the glamorous Anastasia. She was merely a cripple whose image had broken with her back.

Every morning La Rusa awoke, fully expecting the child to have disappeared as miraculously as she had come. It sunk her ageing chest and head in a suffusing sweetness each time she heard the gentle swish of the child's broom across the floor. La Rusa was immune to the reptilian qualities of her new companion; she was aware of, quickly came to love, only her graceful choreography as she swept and reswept the formerly unkempt room. Also the devotion with which the child (whose skills belied her stunted size) manicured aching nails, and tended her body and her hair. La Rusa saw too how this strange creature actually believed all her tales and inventions. Here, at last, was a fellow Russophile and a romantic. Here was a draught of sweetness in her cup of gall. In the absence of any other name, she called the new girl Dulce.

Every day the girls eyed La Rusa's protegée with growing distaste. They stared into her eyes, hoping that it would
drive her back to whatever sunless underworld she had
crawled in from. Had they known how starved the child
had always been of adult love, and how in need of protection she then was, they might have understood that she was
immune to their subtle threats. They laughed at her
uncouth ways and at her astonishment at such things as
inside plumbing, hot water, electric lights, ice and machinery. They teased and bullied her, while she ran willingly
from room to room, polishing shoes and manicuring nails
for these girls who were as strange and fantastic to her as
any of La Rusa's stories.

Gradually, Dulce became so much a part of the Rainbow
that she was as familiar to everyone there as the pattern on
the floor tiles or the stained patchwork quilts that covered
all the beds. Before her accident, La Rusa had insisted on
training her girls not only to be superlative whores but also
to make exemplary wives. So needlework and housekeep-
ing had been a part of each girl's life. And many of the girls
had left the Rainbow to get married. Yet, in the two years
since her fall not a single girl had left. It was almost as
though they were all waiting for her to die so that they
could dig up the floor under her bed and claim their share
of her much talked of fortune.

Since no one left, no new girls came, and the spice of
the unknown was noted and missed by the numerous
clients. It was the only element of change that was ever
referred to. Other things, like the atmosphere of unease,

and the gradual dilapidation of the house, the lack of interest that the girls themselves showed in their work were left
unmentioned. In a world held together entirely by habit
and ritual, no one wanted to be the first to admit to a
change. The old feeling of contentment had given way to
an aura of suppressed aggression. Only the new girl, Dulce,
seemed happy with her lot. It was confusing to call her a
'girl', she wasn't one of the girls at all, she was just a child,
and such a plain strange child at that.

All through the rainy season, when everyone's emotions
mildewed with the inescapable dampness, the men petted
and spoilt Dulce. They brought her sticks of barley sugar
and twists of liquorice, and ribbons for her straggly hair.
What she liked best were emery boards and manicure sets,
miniature scalpels, varnish and polish, anything, in fact,
that could enhance her already beautiful fingernails. Ilario
Gomez, who had a sixth sense for money, was the first to
realise that it was wizened little Dulce with her pond-
dweller's face who was bringing in the clients. She had
found an old usherette's tray in a cupboard and she had
taken to giving manicures to the otherwise dissatisfied
patrons of the house. Ilario Gomez spent many hours
watching her, wondering if her air of innocence were true
or false. Was she really as unaware as she seemed of her customers squirming in their chairs as she caressed their
debauched fingers? He would never understand that she
herself found such exquisite pleasure in the attention of her
nails that any orgasmic writhing would seem to be a natural reaction to her expert probing.

La Rusa missed Dulce when she set off with her tray of tools to do the rounds of the clients' hands. She began to daydream about a different life for her and Dulce, some- where far away from the Rainbow. She also began to complain less about her plight, and even to enjoy herself again. She realised that her greatest pleasure had really been in the fabricating of her stories. She had created a mystery that could only exist if other people believed in her fan- tasies. Dulce believed her so completely that she herself dreamt of the Russian Steppes covered as she knew they were with the scrapings of a million refrigerators and patrolled by dogs that slink like armadillos and bite like mapanare snakes. She dreamt too of a room higher than all the rooms of the Rainbow put together and streaked with gold where people as beautiful and elegant as La Rusa her- self leapt through the air and never fell or broke their backs. La Rusa need not have worried, Dulce was always anxious to return to her. The pleasure of doing someone else's nails could never compete with the thrill of doing La Rusa's.

Ilario Gomez was only interested in counting up the takings, falsifying the accounts, pocketing the difference and banking the rest. He saw the men surreptitiously taking their pleasure with little Dulce, but he failed to see either the measure of love that was growing between the child and La Rusa, or the measure of hate that was gathering steadily towards them from the other girls. Now that no maintenance took place on the building, the persistent rains were rotting away its fabric, just as the general discontent among the girls was rotting away their common-sense.

From the galleried landing they watched Dulce at work, manicuring their clients into various states of ecstasy. Seeing these faces reminded them of the days when such looks and groans were reserved exclusively for themselves. Even their lovemaking had come to be perfunctory and incomplete. They remembered the times when they used to be happy at the Rainbow. They compared such times to their present, and blamed Dulce, not only for dulling their senses, but also for stealing their youth and even for the mangled state of La Rusa's spinal column.

In the old days when La Rusa was vigilant and patrolled the Rainbow maintaining standards and encouraging her girls to excel, they used to hide in their rooms and plot minor rebellions behind her back. Some of that old thrill returned to them as they locked themselves in a conclave to discuss how best to bring down Dulce. No one dared get rid of her altogether. They had tried, on impulse, to get rid of La Rusa and it had brought nothing but bad luck. They wanted something subtle and nasty, painful but not dangerous: something that would hurt Dulce inside to such a degree that she would lose all her naive power.

The dry season had taken its place on the calendar, and the heat seemed to be so entrenched that there was talk of a drought. Dulce was unused to the heat. She had grown up in the temperate uplands. Although she loved the profusion of flowers and the incessant croaking of tree frogs and the patterns of sunlight that pushed through the window bars and forced themselves into the rooms like dancers on the tiles, she could not sleep. So she moved her bed from the space beside La Rusa's own, away from the photographs of Valentino and Fred Astaire and the Russian émigrés, and slept on a mat on a balcony under the stars.

This decampment made the other girls' trick all the easier to play. Before it began, they were all agreed to take part in the punishing. But when the time came to hold the ether pad over Dulce's broad gash of a mouth and hold down her thin pale body until it was still, one of the gang refused to continue.

'It's like killing her,' she said.

'Don't be stupid, Sofia, it's just a lesson, and how come you're so squeamish? When it comes to killing I've seen you try your bit; and don't forget it.'

'It's just that she's only a kid.'

'Then she should act like one . . . Didn't you get enough thrashings when you were one?'

Next morning Dulce woke up with a heavy head and a strange taste in her mouth but with a familiar feeling inside her. She felt a sense of injustice and she ached the way she had ached at home in the uplands. Every time she remembered that her mother had run away and left her in a burning hut, she felt it, and every time her cousins beat her with her yard broom until all her bones ached she felt it. When the uncle who had taken her into his house to live with his own children turned her out in the night to fend for herself without so much as an explanation she had felt it. It had trudged with her from the cane fields to the town. La Rusa's voice had been the only balm strong enough to make her forget her early troubles. All of Dulce's person was contained between the web of La Rusa's stories and the reality of her own fingernails. Now her arms ached and her hands were weighted.

No violation could have hurt her more than this. She knew, even before she looked that her hands were disfigured. It took a long while for her to focus her frightened eyes on her swollen bloodstained fingertips. Carved across the nails of each hand was the word ZAPA, which means toad. She wanted to cry, but the ache was too great, like the aches of home, it would smother her with its silence. Until Sofia came out to see her and to bathe and bandage her hands, she had no idea that she was a despised usurper. In its way, Sofia's attempt at kindness only hurt her the more. So the girls have done this, she thought, and her mind went a dull black too dense even to allow the frogs or cicadas to penetrate the void.

Downstairs, La Rusa called for her, but Dulce could not hear. Upstairs, the girls were frightened by her trance-like silence and they hovered round her. When she eventually picked herself up from her mat and went down to La Rusa, she found her patron aged and anxious. Despite the other girls' protests and promises, La Rusa believed that Dulce had gone. The child herself, who until she entered that cluttered reliquary of a room had thought all her feelings were dead, ran to the old lady and buried her head in the musk and silk that covered her. Her own bandaged hands seemed suddenly irrelevant beside the greater pain of a life ruined by a snapped spine.

La Rusa, who had managed to overlook the spite involved in her own accident, was now determined to repay the damage to her companion's hands. Under the high-pitched droning of the cicadas and over the buzz of humming birds darting through the papery blossoms of hibiscus and bougainvillaea, there could be heard a continual whispering. Ilario Gomez said that it sounded like the house slowly subsiding on its foundations or the crumbling of wood under the onslaughts of silently drilling worms. La Rusa whispered the sweetness back into her injured child.

'Sometimes,' she murmured, 'the only sweetness in life is to remember your scores: those that are settled and those still to be so. I was wrong, Dulce, to let those girls get away with crippling me. I was a coward and I gave in. But we have debts to pay, now, so listen . . .'

As Dulce listened, she realised how little the loss of her one point of pride was when compared to the atrocity carried out on La Rusa. The lethargy that had threatened to swallow her since the morning when she found her nails ruined could not hold against the surge of rage and injustice that she felt for her friend's injury. The girls must all lose what was dearest to them to atone for the robbery of two such qualities.

'The main thing,' La Rusa told her, 'is total secrecy. We don't want a battle, we want a victory.'

From midday to dusk the sun pulsated on the dusty street, pressing its heat against the peeling walls of the Rainbow. Inside, there was a feeling of uneasiness so great that it seemed to get trapped inside the cornbread and even float on top of the sickly cups of coffee. Only one girl, Sofia, left the house, unable to cope with the tension there. No one could say for sure where she went to, but rumour had it that she had hitch-hiked for ten days to the coast and then tried to reach Trinidad. None of the other girls tried to leave, they were all mesmerised by the thought of La Rusa's gold. Although they had never really believed in her stories, they were convinced that the Romanov millions, or at least a large part of them, were interred somewhere in La Rusa's room. They didn't even discuss the subject. They just knew, intuitively, that it was so. They felt the change in the air, and mistook it in their greed for a sign of the old Madame's weakening.

'The old cow is shuddering in her sleep, she can't have long,' the scout reported.

The clients were discontented as they had never been. The girls themselves seemed obsessed by something so far removed from sex that they even forgot to open their legs when they laid down, let alone fake any pleasure. While their Dulce, their pet, no longer tickled their fingers or held their hands. She had thrown away the usherette's tray and she responded only dully to presents of any kinds. It was clear that she had hurt her hands, but how long would the bandages remain, and how long would they be expected to restrain from their pleasures? What kind of a house was the Rainbow after all?

A week passed by, and then another, and then so many weeks that they got lost in the stifling heat and joined that continuum of time which is divided in the tropics only by rain. But the weather held and Madame, sensing the unrest reach its peak even from the inner sanctum of her web, proposed an outing for the girls and their favourite clients to the waterfall of Trujillito. In the early years, there had been outings, but only to the cinema matinées, the market or the travelling circus. There had never been a real outing with food and a barrel of rum and trucks and drivers.

At seven o'clock in the morning the first of the trucks rattled down the narrow cobbled street outside the Rainbow. The girls, dressed up for once in all their finery, piled in. At seven fifteen, from a discreet corner on the edge of town, twenty-five men in their Sunday best clambered over the sides of a second truck. At eight o'clock, a third one stopped outside the demurely shuttered Rainbow, and two men began to load it with the furniture from inside. The street soon filled with curious gossipers, as truckload after truckload was carted away. By half-past ten the last of the contents had been despatched, and Ilario Gomez had paid the cook and the cross-eyed girl who helped her their paltry wages. Ilario Gomez had not been sorry when La Rusa asked him to organise her flight. He lived on a permanent tightrope between the dread of having his embezzlements discovered and his desire to keep stealing. Since Madame was so graciously leaving without having discovered his years of theft, he lifted her with real tenderness from her bed in the stripped room of the Rainbow to a bed on the back of the last of the trucks. Then he assisted the pale blinking Dulce to her place beside her, patting her thin stiff arm with relief, for he too had begun to have designs on the waif, and he was a family man, and such things weren't right. The lease had, by chance, been due for renewal, so it had been a simple matter to let La Rusa's option drop. The deadline was midday, although the landlord had insisted on flexibility, should it be needed. It took some time for him to grasp that there was a game at stake, and the locks must be changed forthwith.

As the last truck drove away, there were boxes of records in the street curling up with the sun, and there were scattered letters and clothes. During the afternoon, these were all picked over and taken or discarded according to merit. Outside the front door there were twelve patchwork quilts, one for each girl; twelve legacies from the days when they were training to be ladies. Each square had been stitched by their own hands. These last years of neglect had taken their toll, though, even on the quilts, because each one was stained with the vestigial remains of thousands of bought orgasms. Stiff with seed, they crackled in the sun.

Dulce and La Rusa travelled almost as far as the missing Sofia was said to have done, and they took a small house with a verandah covered with climbing plants and humming birds. There were no bars on the windows, and there was no upstairs at all. They lived on La Rusa's savings and on the stories that she spun like fine silk from herself. Sometimes, when the evenings were unduly hot and long, they talked over their flight from the Rainbow and tried to imagine each girl's reaction on finding them gone. They both hoped that the shock would last for a long time. They would have been gratified.

The night of the move and the excursion was one of scandal in the town. There was a crowd gathered and waiting long before the girls got home. As they stood wailing with confusion and anger, the recriminations and cursing increased, the street vendors gathered and began to sell plantain chips and popcorn to the audience. Eventually, the National Guard arrived and hauled the former inmates off the house that they were trying to break into. The next morning they had no choice but to hawk their services around the lesser brothels in the town. Once, any girl from the Rainbow would have been welcomed with open arms, but gossip like a cloud of gnats preceded the girls and there were questions and criticism everywhere.

'I heard there was a mere child working there. Is it true she was so young she could hardly speak?'

Everyone had a different story to tell about Dulce, but in all of them, although the rumours grew, Dulce herself shrank until she was scarcely more than a babe in arms. The less the other girls said about her, the more the curiosity grew, so that, wherever they went and wherever they worked, her name and her flat toad face followed them, until the very colours of the Rainbow ran into one dull blob of ill-conceived slander that sat like a heaviness in each chest. They would never be able to forget her. Every dusk with its ephemeral pink halo reminded them of the once perfect fingertips they had defiled. Dulce's memory was everywhere and it was as insistent as the voices of the tree frogs croaking and gloating through the tropical nights.

Gonzalez

Otto came to Paris a sick man. He had cancer of the throat. The tumour was on his voice box. He said he'd got it because he never stopped talking. One of his many pleasures in life was to criticise. And by that same token, he detected it early on, felt its irritation, and was cured. During the months of his treatment, through the autumn of '92, he wasn't supposed to talk anymore, but sometimes he found the temptation irresistible. The stories that surfaced then, against his doctors' orders, were strange ones. They were the incongruous memories that had literally caught in the throat of an ageing revolutionary in his last exile. Among them was Gonzalez.

'Gonzalez is a common name back there, as common as Rodriguez or Moreno, but there was only one Gonzalez in the Carcel Modelo. He was a legend, a random assassin who thrived on fear. The Carcel Modelo is said to be the roughest prison in South America. We didn't mix much there. The political prisoners kept to themselves upstairs, the other inmates divided up into gangs and factions. It was certainly the toughest prison I've ever known. There were incidents every day: knifings, fights, murders and gangland executions. They sent you there, I suppose, in the hopes that you'd get bumped off in the night.'

Otto smiled, apologising for his compatriots and their ways; it was a sweet, childish smile ending in a tug at his ragged white moustache. His voice rolled on in his soft-spoken Spanish, dropping from time to time to a whisper when his malady got the upper hand.

'Who knows what makes a good or a bad prisoner? At liberty, I've been a rebel all my life, but in prison I've found a way to adapt to the system. Perhaps it's because I've spent so many years of my life in jail; I don't know, but left to myself, I get on with my work there, I study and write. I think, in some ways, I'm a model prisoner.

'Beyond a routine brutality, the wardens didn't have much control in the "Model", it was run by D-Block. No one in their right mind went near this D-Block; if they did go in, they didn't live to get out. By a strange chain of cir-cumstances, I started an afternoon school there, teaching the D-Block lifers literature, history and sociology, and it worked out very well. They began to call me the "Proff". The warders were amazed that I could disappear into that shark tank – at three-thirty in the afternoon – and come out at the end of each two-hour session unscathed. I think the governor agreed to my teaching as a good way of get-ting rid of me.

'After a year, I was friends with all the hardest cons. People would piss themselves with fear if some of those murderers even looked at them through their cages, but they all called me "Proff" and sent me up quarters of rum and invitations to their parties. They smuggled my letters in and out uncensored. Those lifers protected me in their hornets' nest, and they put the word out on me, gathered up stories from my past, embroidered them and made up more. They insisted on treating me as though I'd been the leader of every revolutionary army in the continent since Pancho Villa. They made me an honorary one of them: a hard case, a killer, someone to fear.

'In my second year there, the governor mixed us in: the political prisoners and the others. We had to share lockers. This should have been easier on me than for some of the other politicos, but when you live in shit some of it always sticks. Some of the guards really enjoyed needling us politicos. It wasn't as risky as meddling with the cons. I've never understood why prisoners in Europe go on strike to get political status. Why would you volunteer to be branded as scum? Why ask to be mistreated? Well, there I was, branded but somehow getting by, when some bastard picked me out to share a locker with Gonzalez.

'Gonzalez was in for robbing a bank, but behind him he trailed a string of crimes so perverse that no one knew all the details, yet everyone knew enough to know he was the cruellest son of a bitch in the entire jail. Whenever a corpse appeared unclaimed and virtually unrecognisable, nine times out of ten, Gonzalez was to blame. He kept himself aloof from the others, which suited everyone. There was an aura around him; no one bothered him, no one spoke to him, he was just there, a malign presence with the promise of some future violence.

'Of course I'd heard about him, and I'd seen him a few times. He was tall and wiry with big hands and a stubborn look in his eyes. He had unnaturally big thumbs, strangler's thumbs which he flexed obsessively. He used to narrow his eyes a lot as though selecting his next victim. He didn't talk much, but his grunts were eloquent. When Gonzalez cleared his throat, you felt uneasy. Thank Christ, he never came to my classes, but he'd hover sometimes, nearby, pressing his back against the bars, sneering. I used to imagine him dreaming of sawing through human bones for the fun of it.

'My pupils (all killers in their own right) held Gonzalez in a kind of reverence. They gossiped about his crimes and speculated on his past. He was an endless source of fascination. He was a mutilator, a sadist, a monster.

'Meanwhile, I was coping in the Modelo, doing research for my book on Bolivia, teaching two hours a day, three days a week, minding my own business, and most of all managing to stay alive in that so-called Model Prison where hundreds of inmates were slaughtered every year without so much as an inquiry afterwards. If you didn't make it there, someone else got your stuff and your half of a locker.

'Imagine my dismay, then, when the lists were read out, and I was paired up with Gonzalez. He was slouching in line two rows away from me across the prison yard. The sun was beating down and, as usual, the yard was buzzing with flies and stank like a urinal. I glanced sideways and saw him staring at me with a loathing so strong it made me feel sick.

96

'For the rest of the day, I feigned illness. It was easily done, the whole place was riddled with disease. I stayed in my cell while emissaries from my murderous pupils came up to see me with fruit and food.

'Rivas, "the Pirate", a huge sweaty man who'd had one eye gouged out in a fight and wore a black patch, sat by my bedside for a while. One of the few advantages of being a politico there was a room of my own. While everyone else was crammed into cages designed for four but used for up to 20 prisoners, the politicos slept alone. It was all right to be murdered in the Carcel Modelo, but not to have your mind contaminated by any left-wing propaganda. It seemed, to the likes of Rivas the Pirate, another proof of my hidden machismo that I should live in such luxury above them.

'"Eh, Proffe, thank the lord you're a tough bugger, or Gonzalez would chop you up into little bits and stuff you in that locker! I passed him on the stairs just now. Does he give the creeps! I used to be able to look in a mirror confident that I was the nastiest pile of shit I'd ever come across until I got in here. It's a big league!" He sighed wistfully. "I'm a child, an innocent compared to a brother like Gonzalez; and then, there's yourself, Proff, with all due respect," he said, taking in the four cement walls with his one envious eye, "I've heard a thing or two about yourself . . . What balls!"

'The Pirate gave me an admiring thump on the back which rattled my bones then he left

'I lay and thought, "What balls?" *What* balls? I wasn't a fighter, I'd never been a fighter. I'm a thinker. I was always

97

a strategist. In Cuba, in Uruguay, in Chile and at home. Of course, I've lived through violence, but I myself am not a violent man. And, I suppose because I've been interrogated so often (and none too gently) I have a keen memory of pain. That night, I kept thinking of Gonzalez and I kept thinking of the pain he could inflict on me. Old scars and wounds got the better of me for a while, draining whatever courage I had left into fetid air of an interminable tropical night.

'"Gonzalez, Gonzalez Zz . . ." Even the mosquitoes were saying his name.

'Then, towards morning, I thought: I've survived for fifty years, I've always got by on strategy and bluff. I don't even know Gonzalez, but I know about him, and I'm shit scared of his myth. But . . . I'm Otto, and I too have a myth. Gonzalez doesn't know that the little Proff is terrified, he only knows the myth. If I act tough, I can match his menace, out-macho him and get by again. I told myself, it would be too great an irony to end all my efforts there, in prison, dissected by a mindless maniac.

'It became my goal to make Gonzalez more afraid of me than I was of him. Day by day, we met at our locker; we had no choice within the system – our plastic plates and cups were kept there. I took the initiative on the first morning and set the tone for what were to be long months of playing games. I was oozing aggression: it was genuine, I didn't much believe I'd pull off my scam and I was furious at Gonzalez because he was about to waste away my entire life.

'"So you're Gonzalez," I sneered. He was standing quite close to me, dangling one hand behind his back. I thought, now he'll stick that knife in my guts. I said, "I'm not sharing anything with any son of a sick bitch. This is my jail. I'm the Proff. If you want to die, let's get it over with. I'm in a hurry today, D-Block is waiting. So? Piss-sleeves!"

'Gonzalez jerked his shoulders and blinked slowly, but he didn't move. "There'll be time, Proff, later. I sliced the gizzard out of two bits of vermin last night."

'"And?"

'Gonzalez shrugged.

'Four times a day we went to our locker and swapped stories. Time and again I felt myself unable to compete, even in my imagination, with his profound nastiness. Every day I felt the brazen untruths of my boasts emerge from my mouth like bubblegum. Surely he'd notice the hollowness? I'd always thought you could smell fear and I tried to keep as much physical space as possible between us to distance my own bouquet.

'My relative peace in that prison was wrecked. I couldn't sleep anymore. What I ate curdled in my stomach and drinks crawled like poison around my veins. I found my days slipping into slow motion. I was convinced Gonzalez would find me out; it was only a question of when.

'During those months, my reputation had never been so high with the cons. My shoulders ached from the appreciative blows I kept receiving, "What a Proff!" "What a man!" "What a macho!"

'The last prisoner to share anything with Gonzalez died with his balls cut off. No one knew if the balls bit happened before or after his death. I began to feel a chronic ache in my own balls. They twitched at the mere mention of Gonzalez.

'One day, I remember it was in May and the rains had begun. Torrential, desperate rain machine-gunning down on the iron roofs. My nerves were flayed. I'd slept even less than usual. The inside of my mouth tasted like a latrine and the rum I'd drunk the night before was rocking biliously inside me. The window in my cell was a grid ten centimetres square. I could see a bare cement wall through its iron bars. On the ledge, dead mosquitoes were mounting up. I wondered how many years it would take for them to entirely obscure my view. I watched the rain come down, counting the drops: so many for the hours and days already lost in the Modelo, and so many more for those to come. My last appeal had been turned down, again. So I didn't know if I was in for a month, a year, or the rest of my life.

'I weighed up all three possibilities and I knew I couldn't bear another hour of fear. I'd been able to handle everyone but Gonzalez. It was true, I'd never been a killer, but I hadn't been a coward either. I decided to get it over with, to let him kill me since he must.

'My limbs were weak, but I felt strong and young again when I went down the stairs, following the deafening bell on my way to the lockers. By some miracle, there was no one else there, just me and Gonzalez. I said, "Gonzalez, I'm sick of all this bravado, you may as well know I haven't done any of those things I said. I'm not a killer. I'm not even tough, I . . ."

'Gonzalez stretched his huge hand out and rested it by my neck, his roaming thumb flicked like a lizard across my jugular. "So, allow me to introduce Gonzalez as his long-suffering mother bore him," he whispered.

'I was fractionally collapsed against our locker, and he leant towards me, looked around and then continued to whisper. It took a few moments for his words to make any sense.

'"Gonzalez never had any courage, not even enough to fight back in the Barrio. He had a big mouth, though, and he found out that, against all the odds, it could keep him alive in a world that was way too rough for him. When he got sent here to the Modelo (for robbing a bank, what a joke! I was lifting a wallet outside it, the police came, they said 'hands up', I froze, the two robbers were shot dead, and suddenly Gonzalez is a big man). Well, when they sent him here, he nearly died of fright. The Modelo! They talk about it in the Barrio, it's no laughing matter. No, no, really, it's not funny to live among criminals and have no balls.

'"I tell you, Proff, I was born squeamish. I can't even wring the neck of a chicken, I never could.

'"I was doing OK until you came along. The other cons were all too thick to see through me. It was easy to take the credit for all those corpses, it's easy to talk big. But you, Proff, you were the real danger and then some bastard put me down to share with you. I'm telling you, you should hear the way they talk about you on D–Block – it cuts my blood. Every day I come down here with my balls in my mouth. Every day I think I can't stand it any more. Get it over with, do it, but don't torture me any more."

'Gonzalez and I kept our locker for another six months after that, until I was released. We never really spoke again (it wouldn't have been safe to have been seen laughing together), but our eyes met regularly recognising each other as two of a kind.'

Eladio and the boy

Eladio had water on the brain so they said. His life was a fixed idea and a trail of voices dragging him down. He believed that his eldest son, el Mudo, didn't speak because he didn't want to. For the ten years of his son's silence and the ten years of his own lesion, the two had stayed out on the windy crest of the hill. There, a decade ago, an eagle had knocked Eladio down. He lived in the conviction of the bird's return. When his son spoke, the eagle would come and he would be well again. It was a simple belief, but Eladio clung to it to the exclusion of all others. Only he and the boy knew how important the eagle was, only they understood why they stayed out on the slopes; Eladio, 'the mad man' and el Mudo, the mute.

Each night they would wade back to the mud-lined hut where Eladio's wife and other children lived. Each morning they would rise ahead of the sun and the two would take up their stations, watching and waiting with their necks craned in devotion. Eladio was unusually tall and gangly and his flesh had dried off his bones. He had uncanny, watery eyes. He was the laughing stock of the neighbour-hood, but no one dared interfere with his ways. His long fingers combed the air as though searching for small bodies to mangle. Despite this air of menace, Eladio was harmless, doing nothing but watch and wait for the eagle to come and withdraw its talon from his brain and untie el Mudo's tongue. Eladio was glad that over the years his own neck had grown longer. He could see further across the hills.

No one remembered quite how Eladio Mendoza's convalescence had become permanent. On the hacienda, children of eight worked, and old men of ninety worked, only Eladio was exempt and waiting. No one knew why he was allowed to roam and still eat although he never earned his keep. Some thought that perhaps it was that his presence added a strange new quality to their lives. Others thought, vaguely, that if whatever he was waiting for did come, he would maybe intercede in their favour, coming between them and it, in return for their charity.

Antonio Moreno, the foreman, had been friends with Eladio before his accident, and he understood him better than most. It saddened Antonio to see Eladio lost in his obsession. 'We're too low in the foothills here, compadre Eladio, your bird will never return. A hawk will come, and a buzzard, and the vultures are everywhere, but not an eagle.'

Eladio ignored him, as he ignored everything that was not his mute son or a shadow in the sky. He seemed to know better, he mumbled something about what had happened once could happen again. And the children went on throwing stones.

Eladio and the boy paced the hills, splashing through streams and getting caught in the prickly hairs of the sugar cane. Eladio walked in front with his gaunt face upturned while his son trotted behind him. El Mudo was already fifteen years old but he looked no more than eight or nine. He looked like a small child in his father's wake, standing out in all weathers, man and bait to lure an eagle from the Andean sky.

Eladio coaxed el Mudo like a trainer his falcon, speaking softly to him in a constant patter while the boy jogged along behind him, bound by an invisible jesse. 'You don't want them laughing at you, Mudo,' he whispered. 'They laugh at me, but I could squeeze their skulls in my hand. They're already calling you dwarf, Mudo, but you could show them. You've been silent a long time now: speak, and that'll show them. I know you're waiting, like me. I know you'll talk when the eagle returns. But you must talk first to lure him, Mudo, lure him, you could do it, I know . . .' and his voice lulled into the feathery cane flowers and the fluff of drifting acacia and was lost before it ever reached el Mudo's hearing.

Sometimes Eladio would stop abruptly and the boy would almost trip over him, and suffer himself to be hooded by his father's words.

'What would you say if the bird were here, Mudo, what would you say? Say it now, just a little, just one word, Mudo, to see if he comes.'

El Mudo was the only one who braved his father's stares.

Every day, at six and six, Antonio Moreno saw them on his way to and from work. He lived further round the hill from where they stopped. He watched them, and sometimes he envied Eladio his faith, and sometimes he despaired of his simplicity. And Antonio watched Eladio's wife, the comadre Maria and their eleven children struggling to survive, and he did what he could for them, for old time's sake. When he was drinking with his friends on Saturday nights, they would joke about how Eladio had to be good for something or he wouldn't have so many children.

'They have to be his, as well,' Antonio pointed out. 'The comadre Maria is too thin and worried for anyone else to want her.'

Antonio and his friends were used to laughing at misfortune; it gave them strength to bear more. Some of the workers laughed at Eladio himself, but Antonio didn't, he remembered too well how Eladio'd been before. What a man! He'd once knocked out five cane-cutters from neighbouring San Pablo and never taken a scratch himself. Now only his stretched hands were left dangling and the stare in his eye. His heroic body had wasted, his head had gone blubbery and his eyes watered all the time.

The comadre Maria asked Antonio sometimes what she didn't dare ask her husband. 'Why the eagle?'

Antonio tried to explain but the comadre Maria often seemed as dazed as Eladio. 'Who knows? It's an idea, his only idea. Perhaps the eagle is Eladio as he used to be, perhaps he really does want his mind back with all the missing tracks. The way I see it, it's his Messiah. He has a creed of his own, he believes he has only to wait. You see him, and I see him, but he isn't all there, he lives in another world of biding time. He believes he'll be well again when he sees the creature that has stolen his brain. He believes el Mudo will call the eagle down.'

Maria eyed Antonio suspiciously. 'Has God had a hand in this, compadre?' Her voice had a cradling rhythm at odds both with her raddled frame and her demands. Words rocked out from her cracked mouth with all malice rubbed from them leaving only a kernel of complaint swaddled by her soothing delivery.

'Maybe.'

'Well, if he has, it's typical: he sends that man out every day looking for a bird no one's ever seen in these parts: what's wrong with a chicken, I ask you? Or a parrot? No! It had to be difficult! And how are they supposed to cope up there with the two of them chilled to the marrow, and my poor Eladio with all that air in his bones?'

Her questions gathered steam and multiplied so that no one had time to answer them all, let alone Antonio. Yet she seemed content to cull random replies and then to wait on her wicket fence until the next passer-by could add another fragment to her rambling world.

'If my Eladio stood in need of a hen or even a fighting cock, I wouldn't hesitate to give it to him,' she crooned on, more to herself than to Antonio's retreating back. 'I could surprise him, have the hen ready, or borrow a cockerel from the Big House, shave its legs, sharpen its spurs, trim its neck. There's nothing I wouldn't do to find such a bird . . . Or a duck. I could get a duck. He could get a duck from up there on the hill. Or a humming bird, a butterfly, a red cardinal, a cockroach eater, God knows there are enough birds in this valley for everyone. So why get him stuck on this eagle errand?

'It's so typical of God. He never comes here, he has no idea what it's like and then he starts ordering things that are quite out of the question. If he'd picked on old Benito, he'd be away. There isn't anything Benito can't see when he's drunk. But Eladio isn't like that: he's a true believer.

'When I think of the ducks there used to be on el Hatico; they were breeding them, and geese. Geese so fat a family of ten could feast off one bird for a week! Or a parrot – a talking parrot like that one at the shop that can say "say your prayers you bastard" every time anyone opens the door. No one would have begrudged my Eladio that one, as an offering, even though it took years to train him and they say he's older than old Benito. And old Benito himself told me of another parrot, past Mendoza . . .'

Comadre Maria could talk for hours around her husband's problem casting her net of words as they ebbed and grew in the hopes of catching an audience.

Eladio's hut was so squalid and unkempt that few of his neighbours cared to venture past the cobbled fence of its yard. Offerings of food and leftovers were handed across the rusty wires on banana leaves or in twists of brown paper and gratefully received by the swarm of naked children on the other side. The comadre Maria was a naturally untidy person who had long since given up making any effort to restore order to her domestic chaos. Her one chore was to prepare breakfast for Eladio and el Mudo, which she did religiously, stacking her sacraments into billycans for them to take with them when they left before dawn. Then she spent the rest of the day wandering from hut to hut pursued by her hungry offspring, or she stayed at home, leaning on her rickety fence and waylaying whoever came past her on their way to and from the store.

When she was younger, she had earned her living by cooking meals for the fieldworkers and sending them out across the hacienda, hot in billycans. It had been a good job and one that no one could take from her since she had been famed for cooking the best re-fried beans in the neighbourhood and her maize cakes rose of their own accord as though by magic. Now, though, with her children pestering her like flies, she couldn't seem to satisfy them let alone settle down to anything like work herself. As the children grew older, they wiped their own faces and made themselves dresses and shorts and went out to work. The boys helped carry the cane fibre to furnace the mill and they weeded in between the lines of sugar cane. The girls went into service in the town.

The girls came home once a month with the lice washed from their hair and clean cotton frocks, but with their fingernails bitten to the quick. Their mother didn't notice whether they were worked too hard or not, and Eladio was always out on the hills, so he didn't see how tired and frightened his little girls were. Even when they were ten and twelve and hardened to their duties at the sink and washing board, they still made their pilgrimage home once a month, bearing all their wages to the squalid shrine of their mother's lap. Their first question on returning home to their littered yard and their ragged siblings was always, 'How's father?' and the answer was always, 'He's still the same.'

'It's the air in his bones,' their mother would say. She didn't know what this air in the bones was, but she knew that no one else had it and she'd become proud of it. She and her family might not have any milk tins with herbs and flowers in their yard, and they might not make a new broom every day with twigs stuffed through the cylinder of a sardine tin and keep the house clear, and they might not get as many sardines as their neighbours, or even as many beans. And it was true that she had long since lost the thin reins of her home, but Eladio had air in the bones, which was rare and wonderful, and that gave her life some meaning. She cared for Eladio and el Mudo, they, at least, were fed and clothed. She and the others must make do, they were incidental. Her own bones showed, but what was that compared to having air in the bones?

In the early years of Eladio's illness, there was muttering on the hacienda; no one liked to see a family go to ruin. And at first there was more conjecture about the eagle, but gradually, that too died down. The only eagles they'd ever seen were on the rum bottles in Mendoza Fria. They knew that in the cold uplands of the Paramo the highest point was the Pico d'Aguilar (Eagle's Peak), but none of them had seen that either. Old Benito claimed he'd seen eagles flying over the hacienda in formation when the last dictator came to power, but everyone knew they must have been vultures. You just didn't get eagles on the hacienda. After all, old Benito said he'd once been stampeded by a herd of elephants behind the sugar mill. The dictator had been keen on vultures, he imposed a fine of five bolivares for anyone who stole a vulture's egg: he said vultures kept the countryside clean. Between them, Benito and Eladio were turning the hacienda into a jungle. All in all, the other workers let them be. Benito had nearly a century of rot gut rum on his brain, and Eladio had been trepanned by his fall. Clouds came in through the back of his head and pushed rain water out through his eyes. So if Eladio chose to summon down rum labels from the sky, let him! It could have been worse, he could have been calling down wolverines or mapanare snakes.

Eladio wasn't from the estate that he lived on. He had been born over a hundred miles away in the uplands. He'd been in some kind of trouble there and had come as a young man, looking for work. Antonio Moreno had seen the use of such a giant and had taken him on (urged too perhaps by a sense of kinship in the fact that his own wife, Zara, was also a foreigner on the hacienda). No one really trusted a person if he didn't have relatives for generations born on the same piece of land. Eladio had stayed and married Maria, making his home in a disused mud hut that huddled up against the ruins of a former estate house. The other workers looked on him uneasily, admiring his prodigious strength, but never really accepting either him or his children. He had no roots and no history. And now, worst of all, he had no memory; or so the workers thought. But Eladio could remember the highlands.

He remembered being sent to work as a boy, and how the rough unbroken handle of his new machete had blistered his hand until it bled. He had bandaged the crease with cool palm fibres and rags. The shreds had chafed the wound as he worked on until his hand was stiff. He remembered how he had gone home and wept to his father, begging him to let him rest, and how his father had beaten him until every bone seemed swollen. And he remembered running into the hills past the patches of potatoes and strips of oats and barley; he had stumbled on and up over the outcrops and on to a crag. That was where he first saw the eagle's nest.

It had been sheltered by overhanging thorns from intruders. Eladio had cut a secret trail through the steep rock scrub to the eyrie and he returned there every night. He had watched them pair and breed, hunt and return. He had learnt to live with his work and then to excel like the king eagles he came to worship.

Eladio came to be accepted. He could lie only his body's distance away from the clawed feet of the two harpies. He took them gifts, and they came to accept them too. They ate his smell on the ruffled feathers of smaller birds. They began to look on him as a benign part of the landscape, approaching their nest unchallenged. They did not bother to change their plucking post when Eladio came near. He watched them on their hunting forays, soaring over the valley on an upcurrent of air and then gliding with their wings trimmed in perfect balance. He learnt to stare with their large eyes boring into their prey. He stretched and flexed his own fingers until his one-handed grasp could kill both hawk and hare. He began to stroke the ridge of bone on his brow compulsively.

Through the unvarying chill of the upland air, he watched the harpies hover and dive. He watched them moult: grey feathers for more grey feathers and the six black bars on their tail. He watched their hooked bills at work, tearing flesh and limbs. The waving of their crests then was the grey crown of their sovereignty over the whiteness of their chests. He spent all his free time in the litter of their prey, lying steeped in the fur and feet of innumerable victims. His nest was their pellets. For four years he told no one about the harpies.

He had made a friend at work of another boy his own age and they began to spend most of their time together. They chose to stand side by side in the hoeing lines and work together sharing their planting and gathering. They shared their lunches of boiled potatoes and hot peppers, their wheat cakes and their guarapo. They found each other presents and told each other secrets. But Eladio couldn't bring himself to share his eagles. His friend, however, was sure there was something, and he would not be refused. He bantered and pestered and teased Eladio day after day.

'What's so important that you can't tell me, Eladio?' he would ask. 'What have you got to hide? Who have you got? If it's a girl I won't betray you. Aren't I good enough to share your secrets? Why can't I know?'

Eladio sensed that to tell would be to betray.

'Don't be so mean, Eladio, tell me what you know, where you go. I've seen you sneaking off. Tell me,' his friend would wheedle.

Eladio refused. He refused a hundred times a day, so often, in fact that it soured his friendship. He was afraid, but he couldn't bear not to go and see his bird-shrine in the hills.

It was early September and in the market town of Timotes there was to be the last fair before the rains set in. For two years running Eladio and his friend had gone together, setting off at dawn to walk the fifteen miles cross country. That year, Eladio's friend announced that he had arranged to meet a girl there and would be going alone. As soon as his chores were done, Eladio himself set off for the eyrie, confident for once that he would not have to give anyone the slip on his way through their scattered hamlet. So it was the one day he was not on his guard as he made his way through the tangled undergrowth to the eyrie. Once out on the crags, Eladio unwittingly led the way, stepping over the debris of splintered skulls by the plucking post and over the scattered pellets to the nest itself. Silently, his friend had followed him and Eladio climbed through the scrub, so deep in thought that he hadn't even heard the occasional furtive rustling behind him. Nor had he seen his enraged friend struggling breathlessly at his back. He hadn't seen him getting more and more puzzled as he climbed, so sure was Eladio of being alone. He didn't know that his friend was there, nervously fingering the heavy thongs of a catapult in his pocket.

There was only one eagle in the nest. She was brooding while her mate was out hunting. As Eladio neared the eyrie, something changed. The harpy reared up and flew at Eladio, reaching furiously for his head. She trimmed her wings and braced her legs, talon outstretched for the kill. Eladio called to her above him, in a loud soothing voice, 'It's only me.'

His friend saw the bird's feet ready to tear open Eladio's skull and he fired the stone that he had been holding ready in his hand. He aimed at her head and his aim was good, he had had years of practice. The eagle shuddered and crashed to the ground, writhing spasmodically. Eladio crumpled to his knees, bowing down over the twitching eagle. The fear that his friend had felt for him fled and was overshadowed with all his other fears (of darkness of knife fights of the Wild One) by the fear of Eladio's lament. It echoed across the hills and valleys of the uplands, curdling every thought and feeling but the instinct to run away. And so he ran, crashing and tumbling back down the path and as far from the demented wail as his short legs could take him.

Eladio couldn't remember what happened during the following month, he knew only that he never went home again and that his slippered feet took him downwards into a landscape of heat and trees and when the woven cotton of his shoes rotted away his bare feet led him on until his hunger took him to the Hacienda el Hatico where Antonio took him on.

As Antonio said, there were no eagles on the hacienda, it was too low for them. The years passed lost in work and the births of Eladio's first three children. He was noted mostly for his strength and his reserve. He spoke very little to anyone, reserving most of what he had to say for the ears of his eldest son. The child followed him everywhere, trundling along behind his father, or holding his hand, prattling to him while he worked. Behind his back, people surmised that Eladio was a man with a tragedy in his past, but given his physique no one had ever dared ask him what that tragedy was. Only the most serious trouble could drive a man away from the land he was born on. There was gossip of murder, patricide and all the other crimes beloved of strangers. Eladio was unmoved by the surrounding curiosity; he kept his guilt and his grief to himself, content to spend his days with his eldest boy, to work in the cane fields and then to return to Maria with her business of billycans and babies.

Antonio Moreno still remembered the day the one and only eagle was sighted over the hacienda. El Mudo was five at the time and, it being a Saturday afternoon, Eladio and the child were sitting out at the highest point of the hill over the creek watching the other workers making their way to the distillery on the farside of the hill. Antonio himself was headed there; they always went on Saturday nights. What else was there to look forward to if not to get drunk once a week? Only Eladio never drank, preferring to chatter with his son.

It came first as a distant line in the sky and then grew and grew until its shadow seemed to cover the hill. Eladio was on the hilltop calling and waving. The eagle glided towards him with a wing span as wide as a kitchen rafter. From down below, Antonio could see Eladio's wild dance. When the eagle passed he turned away, embarrassed for his friend and his strange antics. He followed the eagle as it disappeared again into a black bar on the horizon. It didn't circle and it didn't return. All was quiet on the hilltop so he made his way to the distillery and soon lost Eladio from his thoughts.

Later that evening, when they found Eladio with his head broken open and his child struck dumb beside him, shivering on the hillside, no account could be given. Later still, when Eladio, at least, regained his powers of speech, he babbled endlessly about having been struck down by the bird, but Antonio knew that wasn't true. The eagle had soared high over his friend's head, and whatever fall he suffered he suffered alone.

For over a year Eladio's head was bandaged. His eyes acquired a half-savage stare and wateriness of extreme old age. His flesh began to waste and his mind was gone. As for el Mudo, it was generally assumed that once the shock of seeing his father fall and crack open his head was over, the child would talk again. Months passed and then years and neither man nor boy recovered from their shock.

In the ten years since the accident, the story of Eladio's fall was embroidered and changed, picked open and re-woven with endless variations. No one really remembered the details anymore and no one remembered how little had ever been known, but they all agreed that Eladio and his dwarfed disciple had a special mission and no one stood in their way as they waited for the eagle's return.

A feeling for birds

Love came and chopped up Nunzia's heart like a handful of parsley on a marble slab. The knife it used was a mezza luna, a half-moon blade that rocked, in the end, from its own propulsion. It was a two-handled knife so thorough it turned fibre to pulp. Nunzia's sister, Ana, kept caged birds on the balcony outside their shared bedroom. She had a lark, a brown blackbird and a pied wagtail. In her time, Ana had rescued chaffinches, sparrows, swifts and starlings, a wren, a robin, and, albeit briefly, a young barn owl.

It was said in the village that Ana had miraculous hands. She could bestow the gift of life on ravaged birds, splint broken wings, and unglaze the button eyes of frightened birds pulled from the mouths of callous cats and dogs. Nunzia shared her sister's big feathery double bed, and she shared the household chores, gossip and outrage, jokes, and the occasional thimbleful of thick black walnut liqueur, but she had never shared her feeling for birds. Never, that is, until she found a hybrid somewhere between a lark and a nightingale, trapped in her own unsuspecting and volumi-nous breast. For, ever since she had met Domenico, a bird had been flapping and fluttering uncontrollably inside her.

123

Nunzia would have liked to have told her sister about it, let her bring its startled wings to order, calm its racing heart; but she sensed that this bird, so chaotic and unasked for, would be the only one to pine and die between her sister's magic fingers. It was taken for granted by all of the eleven brothers and sisters of the Rossi family that Nunzia alone was immune to either love or lust. She was the youngest daughter, and her place was at home. There was no place for strangers in her life until Domenico came along. Love, for Nunzia, was what other people felt; she rose and fell on its tides vicariously, following the good and the grim marriages of her brothers and sisters, and following the contortionist twists of the soap operas that ran for years, quickening her blood from 1.40 p.m. to 2.20 p.m. from Monday to Friday. Nunzia lived in a small landlocked village buried deep in the Umbrian forests. She never went further afield than the market town. She never met anyone new and never socialised beyond the immediate circle of her vastly extended family.

Domenico had left the village twenty years before when Nunzia was still a child. He was an only son made good and working in Milan. At New Year, Easter, and the Feast of San Crescentino, he returned and touched base, cruising his big car and his city clothes past the vineyards and vegetable plots of the village. Domenico in the countryside was a fish out of water, and Nunzia, like the good Umbrian she was, didn't like fish, didn't notice them. Domenico breathed the rarefied air of a foreign city, wore suits and a collection of silk ties as varied as her own brothers and sisters.

They were two people made invisible to each other by circumstance. He had never noticed her, nor she him until the day when the bell tolled for old Cenci's funeral. Nunzia had found herself on Buona Vita street marooned from her car by the surge of funeral goers, jostled by the black-clad crowd, pushed forwards into the path of Domenico. They collided, soft bosom to silk-lined chest. Nunzia blushed, Domenico smiled, and with his smile, followed by a grey-eyed gaze, the startled bird was born.

No one noticed as they trudged after old Cenci's coffin, no one saw. Only she and Domenico, secret in the crowd, began a love affair in the way it was to be continued: with a shopping bag between them held tightly in Nunzia's stubby but manicured hand, a bag of bait to lure the foreign falcon to her nest. They began to communicate through signs and whispers, stealing minutes out of the day.

Their first proper meeting took place later that day imbued with an urgency and a secrecy that Nunzia found thrilling. How could Domenico have known that out of a casual piece of luck he would unleash such long pent-up passion? They met and made love behind the disused church on the hill above the village, sheltered from prying eyes by a bank of sweetly scented broom.

All through the remainder of the evening, while Nunzia prepared a dense paste of three types of meat and nutmeg for the ravioli she would make on the following day, the bird inside her sang all the tunes she had ever heard and others that were new and alarming.

Then, each day from Monday to Friday, between the

soap opera and supper, Nunzia slipped out, escaping for anything from twenty to forty minutes for another episode on the hill, or behind the football pitch, at the tobacco shed down by the river, in a lay-by beside the shrine of the Madonnina, and once almost to be discovered under the walnut tree that marked the entrance to the olive grove at Nuvole. They conversed very little, beyond endearments which they had both stockpiled over the years and wearied of ever finding anyone to lavish them on. Domenico's fair Etruscan face masked a fastidious pride in his elevated station. He was given to quoting Dante and Carducci in cryptic phrases curtailed, he said, for being perhaps too sophisticated for Nunzia, implying though that nothing could really be too sophisticated. Nunzia, who spoke mostly the thick dialect of the village, had no idea what sophisticated meant, nor did she care. Her immediate pleasure and its lingering aftermath had transformed her life. It was only after Domenico went away again, back to the mists of Milan, that she began to dwell on the meaning of the word. During his absence, she was sustained by the knowledge of what she had done and the hope that he would return sooner than usual and thus acknowledge the reciprocity of their need.

Their affair remained secret, and secretly Domenico felt guilty, but Nunzia herself had no desire to marry. Having lived in close proximity to many marriages, to be wed was the last thing she wanted. She longed for romance and something of her own. Kneading the seemingly endless heaps of flour and eggs, she was above suspicion. Nobody knew of the yearning that she folded into her dough with the egg yolks from her sister's hens. Nobody knew as she scanned the back pages of coloured magazines for recipes that she had found a way of caressing herself in the kitchen. She began to concoct strange dishes, the stranger the better as far as she was concerned. She knew intuitively from the slight curl of Domenico's lip under his pale moustache that nothing could really be too elaborate and different for his taste. Theirs was a love affair of touch and taste. When he was absent, she learned to taste him in the alien flavours of foreign food.

Nunzia was the family chef. She shopped and cooked, twice a day no matter what, preparing the same things over and over again with the unvarying touch that was the pride of the village. The family ate as their grandparents had eaten, differing only in the richness and quantity of the food now that the days of poverty had been swept away. Only food grown and reared within the parameters of their own backyards had ever been considered fit to eat. Then suddenly, Nunzia, who had never stepped out of line, turned their house into a witches' cauldron and threatened to starve them all to death, serving fish instead of pork or rabbit, and birds with names they had never heard which she dredged up from some supermarket in Castello. She spurned the simple trinity of herbs from their garden – the parsley, rosemary and oregano – and began to introduce extraordinary flavours to wreck their dinners and sabotage their digestion.

Nunzia's family's surprise turned to pity and then to

anger to no avail. She had set her course for collision with all that was good and comforting. She slaved over her chopping board, working the mezza luna from morning till night, chopping and slicing all her new foods with a gusto that no one could explain.

Nunzia had a friend in the village who had lived for years in the South of France and knew a hundred secrets of French cuisine. Although these secrets had lain dormant for decades – no one would want to eat French food when they could have their own – she was happy to show Nunzia how to prepare the most complicated sauces, glazes, stuffings and coulis.

Domenico made an unscheduled visit to the village in October, staying only two nights, but seeing Nunzia on each of them. He whispered that he missed her and she was content. He would be back for the New Year, he told her. She invited him to dine with her family then; she would find a pretext. The winter seemed almost too short for her as she perfected a menu to impress him.

Every time Nunzia prepared one of her 'pondlife plates' as her brothers called them, or trussed up cuts of meat that most local households wouldn't have thrown to their dogs, there was always some kind of placebo in the guise of the plain homemade pasta they loved with a sauce of ripe tomatoes, basil, garlic and fresh oil, a salad picked from the village byways, and a roast chicken or grilled pigeon taken from their own roost. So the new things sat and steamed on the big round table, untouched by anyone but Nunzia herself who chewed them with an ecstatic expression on her face. Day by day, the remains of her new efforts were consigned to the rubbish bin.

However, when Domenico struck up a sudden friendship with Nunzia's brother Piero and invited himself round for dinner on New Year's Day, the family felt obliged to taste some of her dishes. In vain had Piero warned her not to insult his guest with her new-fangled messes. Instead, she excelled herself, serving seven courses of inedible and unpronounceable things. Even the chicken was ruined in some bought wine. Even the wines of which their cellar was full had been replaced as though by alchemy by stuff from the supermarket that was bound to poison them, being French. The shame was hard to bear. Each of them knew that Nunzia used to be such a good cook: she knew how to pluck and gut and truss a bird better than any woman in the village; she was an expert roaster, a genius at a ragu sauce. The taste never varied, not from one year to the next, and now, suddenly, she had gone mad and needed trussing herself in a straitjacket.

They wanted to apologise, but Domenico cut in, pretending that he liked the food. He said it was sophisticated, and Nunzia smiled, showing the dimples in her smooth and youthful face.

'Too damned sophisticated,' Piero muttered, gagging on a forkful of sole joinville. He had seen her putting the shells from the prawns in it earlier in the day. He didn't like to think what else was in it. Poor Nunzia and poor them, he thought. Where would it end?

After that dinner, Nunzia relaxed. She limited her torture

by foreign food to Sundays. For the rest of the week, she cooked and cleaned with a contentment that no one could understand. She sang to herself, often; and she began to talk to Ana's birds in their cages. Everyone on Buona Vita street had said that the strange cooking fad would pass, and they'd been right, it almost had. Sunday lunch was an ordeal they learnt to bear with grace. After all, poor Nunzia had no pleasures in her life. Meanwhile Nunzia liked being pitied, it made the bird flutter inside her. She kept her secret year after year. He had increased his thrice yearly visits to the village to six, funnelling enough passion to satisfy his hidden mistress.

At forty, Nunzia had grown overweight, and her thick black hair would have been streaked with grey if she hadn't dyed it. She spent more time talking to the birds than following her soap opera which everyone thought showed how she was growing old. She made herself half sick with excitement on Saturday nights and Sunday mornings preparing the ritual feast and she made her family half sick trying to eat it; but somehow a balance was struck. Where once she had known only a dull ache, she now held a secret that let her soar over the fields at will. She still loved Domenico, and she loved her secret. Sometimes she didn't know which she loved more: her occasional lover who lived on the edge of the earth, or the sense of herself, of Nunzia, the mistress of touch and taste.

Silvio and the washing lines

'Rumbling, tumbling, mumbling . . . tra la, grumbling, shaking, aching . . .'

Silvio lay in his thin iron bed shaking through the third cycle. It was Monday and his room had been rattling for almost an hour. His wife, Dina was snoring loudly on her bed on the other side of the room. He watched her covers tremble. Downstairs, in the basement cantina, his daughter, Graziella was doing the weekly wash. The third cycle was always the most violent. It only lasted for five minutes, but it vibrated their large breeze-block house with the force of the earthquake of 1917. The fourth was noisy too, but it didn't shake.

Silvio was eighty-four and had the diminutive frame of a frail child. He was, he knew, singularly mismatched in shape and size for his gargantuan wife, but until her stroke it had been his pleasure to wallow in the receptive billows of her flesh. If he concentrated hard, on Monday mornings, he could still feel aroused to see her tremble in her sleep, propelled by the churning machinery below them. On other days, he rose early, lighting the small fire in the sitting room with twigs and broom before shaving and applying lemon-grass lotion to his cheeks, ritually sleeking his hair and then changing from his grey woollen vest and long johns into his day clothes by the new fire's crackling heat. But Mondays were different; they filled him with nostalgia. He lay in bed and thought of all his decades of past pleasures and of the past.

If it hadn't been raining, he could have opened his shuttered window, leant out, and watched Graziella hanging out the washing, methodically pegging out the strings of sheets and vests and clothes across their allotment. She had a system, Dina's system, from left to right above the vegetables and across the cane fence of his flowers. He had always liked to watch this hanging out; he felt a sensual delight at the thought of clean almond-scented cotton and soft socks; fresh, aired sheets and spotless tablecloths. He himself was scrupulous in his habits and dapper in his dress. He spent hours every day preening himself for his ritual aperitif at the local bar. First Dina and now Graziella ensured that his clothes were always immaculate. Listening to the washing machine chugging around brought back to him images of the past, recalling the days when the site of their house was still a vineyard, and the village was still a huddle on the hill.

It was raining hard. It had been raining for days, drumming down on the roof and balcony, soaking into the mud, beating the russet leaves off the surrounding oak trees at last. It had even temporarily filled the river again. Silvio had lost count of time except from day to day and to tally his age, so he didn't know if it was ten or twenty years ago since the sound of the river beyond the village had faded. Before it dwindled, though, he could lie in bed and listen to it rushing by, and on Mondays, he could hear the rhythmic pounding of clothes on stone as Dina and the women from the village beat out their washing. He had liked to watch them then from his old room, propped on a stool so he could reach the high narrow window sill, resting on his elbows as he stared out across the valley. The washing machine might be easier, and its rhythm was strangely disturbing, but washing day used to be more satisfying when half the women knelt prone by the river. What a line up of backsides that had been! And nearer still; the other women gathered around their iron cauldrons, boiling sheets in ash-water, filling the air with the thick, distinct smell of wood ash and hot soiled linen coming clean. The girls used to hitch their long skirts up high and roll up their sleeves and glisten with sweat as they stirred the cauldrons and stoked the bonfires under them.

The hanging out was still the same, though; a link between the past and the present. But Graziella wouldn't be hanging anything outside today because it was raining. He could hear her stomping back up the stairs, muttering to herself. She'd be annoyed at not being able to get everything dry. It was seven o'clock. It would take her a good half hour to regain her temper. Silvio decided to stay out of her way; he'd have his coffee later. He'd pretend to go back to sleep. If she looked in, he'd just lie still and breathe gently and regularly with his face turned to the wall. The sound of the rain was tiring. Each drop seemed to tap on his nerves, stirring up his memories, muddling things and wearing him out. Suddenly, he felt so confused that, unawares, he slept.

He was awoken an hour later by Graziella's screaming.

'O Dio! O God! O God! Help! Everyone help! Babbo, babbo, come quickly!'

Silvio was babbo, the father of nine children all grown up and bigger than himself. In his old age, he had become marginalised in the family; treated, he often thought, almost like a child, petted and scolded by turns as though age had somehow made him incompetent when really he had now become more conscientious than ever. While Dina was up and about and in charge, she had protected him, keeping his position at the head of the family surrounded by an aura of enforced respect, despite his little eccentricities. But now that she was relegated to a wheelchair and grew fatter and fatter and daily more plaintive, he had lost both his place and his role. His family never seemed to need him now; they humoured him, he knew. Sometimes, when he was late up from his workshop, he even suffered the indignity of not sitting at the head of the table.

So when Graziella cried out to him, he was alarmed. Only disaster could have sent her back to him; back to her childhood when she used to call him in her need. He tumbled out of bed and struggled into his clothes, fumbling with his shirt buttons, cursing, for once, their meticulous ironed folds, tearing one of the buttons off in his efforts to get dressed too quickly. He heard the button rattle under his bed, bouncing on the parquet floor. Silvio paused, guiltily; he'd get into trouble now. He promised himself he'd retrieve the button and sew it back on secretly, so that Graziella wouldn't nag him about it. But time, which had been so leisurely all his life, had concertinaed and her voice had been joined by some of his other children's. Something was wrong. Something terrible, and Graziella was wailing in dismay.

Behind him, Dina was stirring angrily, complaining about the noise. He pretended not to notice and went out into the chill white corridor to investigate. His family was on the stairs to the cantina. He found them there, watching a surge of flood water gurgle up towards them. Licio, his youngest, was stripping his clothes off to the waist. Silvio watched his son's balding pointed head descending to the water. Silvio felt a chill in his bones.

'What are you doing? Where are you going?' he asked faintly, afraid both by his question and at any eventual reply.

'The cantina's flooded, babbo. All the wine's down there, and the wool for the factory. I've got to get it out.' Silvio watched his son shudder as he waded down the remaining steps into the water and disappeared through the basement doorway into the muddy tide. He called after him, 'Licio . . . Where are you going, Licio?'

They had called him, but only to bear witness; no one had any time for their father. Silvio's call remained un-answered. He felt himself staring after Licio: a tall, skinny man shrinking back into a little boy. Licio couldn't swim. None of them could swim. Water was for washing in. He'd

137

drown. Silvio felt his eyes tighten with anxiety. He had nine children, six daughters and three sons, and now he was losing Licio to the underworld.

The others were talking all at once. They always did, shouting each other down, shouting at him. There was no ill will in their hubbub, just confusion. Their words blocked at his deafness, at the silence that shoved him further and further back into his own world. Their mouths moved like landed trout. Behind him, from his bedroom, he could still discern Dina keening for her morning wash, summoning her daughters in a series of moans. They had all inherited their mother's voice: a loud bellowing that had surrounded him for more years than he could remember.

'Wine' 'Wool' 'Wood' 'Ruined' 'Water'

'Graz-i-ellaaa! Graz-i-ellaaa!'

'Stores-wine-wood!'

Licio re-emerged, pushing a battered oak barrel of wine in front of him which the others hauled up. Licio was blue with cold, but he turned back and disappeared again. Then he returned on trip after trip, guiding other barrels, boxes and crates to the safety of the stairs. The water neither rose nor receded. It came up to his neck in the cantina, and he waded through it, flailing his bare blotched arms at the floating contents of their store rooms. On one trip, he came spluttering up with the washing machine bobbing in front of him on its side. They had been joined by neighbours now, and between them they hauled the cumbersome machine up the six stairs to the hall. After half an hour, the flood had begun to subside, and Licio was joined by his sister; together they thrashed through the floating debris and retrieved things.

Baccharini, their next door neighbour, was standing next to Silvio, commiserating with him. The stream had flooded up behind the cemetery and diverted itself down the hill and turned into the lower ground of Buona Vita Street. Five of the houses there had been flooded, but Silvio's was the first and had taken the brunt of the inundation. The Fire Brigade were on their way to pump out the cantinas. It was the rain. It was bad luck. He was sorry about the workshop, sorry about it all. He squeezed Silvio's shoulder and backed up the steps to the water-logged street to his own house and his own damage.

Silvio leant against the wet cement wall and stared. The damp was slowly seeping up his corduroy trousers, it had nearly reached his groin. For half an hour he had been as paralysed as his wife, but now a word had sunk in: 'workshop'. His new workshop was in the cantina. Sixty years of amassed tools and bits and pieces were down there underwater. His manuscripts were there, his wood carvings and all that comprised his trade as shoemaker. A sound tried to surface from his throat but couldn't, then he began to move down to the doorway, jerking his arms and legs in spasms like a toy soldier. Those nearest to him tried to bar his way, but he pulled himself free and sunk into the water. He was only four foot ten, and the flood still came up waist deep on him. His workshop was in the far corner of the cantina, by the side entrance where the errant stream had burst in.

139

From behind a stack of kilner jars, Graziella screeched out to stop him. He was delicate, he'd get pneumonia. The rescue workers paused in the water to watch, but they ignored Graziella and let him glide on, pushing through the water to his drowned nest. They had hauled out much of the stored spools of wool, the wine, the hams, the washing machine, the gallons of vinegar, the crates of parquet for the unfinished floors, so that most of what was left was firewood, loose wool, and bottled vegetables. All that they had stored up against want was warped or muddy or lost.

As Silvio forced his way through the receding tide, parting the water on his way to his own private haven, they realised for the first time that he had lost the essence of his whole world there, and some of it would have to be retrieved for him. So they followed in his wake to help salvage what they could of his tiny crammed domain. When Silvio reached his workshop door, he was unable to shift it. It was Licio and the men who forced it open, releasing a torrent of mud that knocked them backwards.

Six foot by four, the underground room was stacked from floor to ceiling like a venerated shrine. Rows of tools covered the walls like votive candles. Much of the clutter was his miscellaneous collection of tools and mementoes, both useful and occult but all fouled with slime. His strips of leather and twine, olive wood for whittling, knives, scalpels, nails and lasts had been thrown from their stylised display into a tangled heap. Silvio stood trembling in the midst of it, his fine white hair shaking on his head and his teeth chattering uncontrollably.

140

Licio and his older brother, Secondo, led their father out, dragging him through the uninvited lagoon like a stunned seal. They pulled him to the relative safety of the outer doorway and up into the unrelenting rain where the firemen had just arrived, glistening in their uniforms, and full of conflicting instructions. Two firemen strode forward and took the old man, lifting him under his shoulders like a child, swinging him up over the thick mud to the road. A crowd of neighbours then took him over, carrying his bird-weight round the front of his house, then hauling the bedraggled owner up the stairs to the first floor and the fire. Silvio was dried and changed, warmed and cosseted, but nothing they could do or say could keep him there.

In galoshes and a clear plastic cape, he went back to his cellar. The firemen had reduced the water to a thick layer of sludge. All his nine children had come to help pick over the losses, sifting through the dregs, chattering and screeching, buzzards and starlings diving at the encrusted mud.

By midday, the rain stopped for the first time in a week, and a pale sun crept into the garden. Every bush and tree was used to hang out the sodden debris from the cantina. The cane wicket around Silvio's flowers was crowned with spools of wet wool. Inside, Secondo and Licio and two of their neighbours were struggling with a huge cardboard box, cursing and laughing out at its unexpected weight:

'This is worse than the washing machine!'

'Dear God, I'll rupture myself if we don't rest for a bit.'

'What the hell is it?'

They dragged it out into the uncertain sun. It was Silvio's box of manuscripts. He was the village bard, the recorder of events. He had written poems in their native Umbrian dialect for all the events that had taken place in the village since he was a boy. Births, deaths and marriages were all celebrated by him. Love and loss, war and pestilence, hail and blights had all been distilled into his rhyming couplets. He'd paid back interest on his borrowed enjoyment of life by making up those verses.

When he wasn't composing, or sipping aperativi at the bar, or smoking his thin cheroots and holding forth on the moon and the stars and all the forces of nature to his fellow villagers, he worked as a shoemaker. But he had always been a dilettante at heart: a poet and a dilettante. He made and mended shoes, but he preferred to shape words out of every day and to carve wood and stone from the valley into little things to give away. And every year, he grew flowers in a corner of the family vegetable plot to present to his friends and admirers and to the girls he admired. He'd been born a peasant, a contadino, but he had an aesthete's soul, the delicate sensitive soul of a poet and a gentleman.

Dina and his nine children had gone hungry time and again because Silvio had never had the heart to drudge as all his neighbours had during the hard years after the war. He'd always been like a songbird in a chicken run. Once his children had grown up, though, they had redressed the balance, working hard and pooling their earnings, making the family well to do, supporting their parents in the style that Silvio had often yearned for. His shoemaking was a hobby now, and one that they all indulged. His carving and his flowers, his cobbling and his poetry kept him busy and out of their way. It was they who had saved to build the new house, and moved them all from the squalid two-up-two-down stone croft in which they had grown up. And Silvio's new workshop had been their present to him, replacing the stone cave under the old croft that he had made his own. He spent ten hours a day there, writing and whittling, making toys and ornaments, olive clogs and spoons. He loved to lure visitors down to his den, and occasionally, when there were leather shoes to be mended, and no one was in a rush to get them back, he still mended them, scrawling poems on their insoles, dedicated to whomever they belonged. Silvio's was a close-knit family. The children were proud of it; it was how they had survived. The bitterness of their childhoods had been all but forgiven, and they protected their father like a rare prodigy: a wayward, gifted child unsuited to the real world. Now that there was food on their table and more in the cantina, who else was a poet on Buona Vita Street?

The box of papers was pulled clear of the mud, and the pages of Silvio's poems were hung out to dry, leaf by leaf on the washing line. Next to them, hanging heavily, were the dozens of pornographic magazines that he had collected over the decades and in which his own writings had been interleaved. The glossy pages of erotic pictures had glued together with the sludge and run, and they hung in sodden chunks over the line, pegged up, from left to right, by Graziella and her sisters. His poems had run and smudged

143

into mascara streaks and the weak heat imprinted them with what looked like lipstick stains from the magazines.

Silvio sat on a terracotta urn and watched his life's work and his life's savings being strung up. They filled all three lines. Then he took his delicate head in his frail hands and held it tightly like a thin china bowl about to fall and break. He stared into the soiled leaves in the winter sun until his eyes blurred with tears. His neatly pressed clothes were spattered with mud, his plastic cape was awry and his soft pink cheeks were as faded as the damp ink. Nothing anyone said or did touched his despair. He kept himself propped on his terracotta perch late into the evening, weeping silently through his fingers at the laden washing lines.

The festa

Maria never went to the festa, she hadn't been for over twenty years. She could see all the preparations and the festa itself from her kitchen window, but she never went down to join in the fun. She always knew what would be served at the banquet because some of the baking was done on her own wood stove, and she often made the meat sauce for the tagliatelli herself, since that was her speciality, but she never went down to take her place at one of the long trestle tables to eat it. She could remember, just after the war, when she was a girl, how she used to walk down from Zeno Poggio on the crest of the hill to join the procession of la Madonnina. She used to walk down with her sisters and their friends, jostling to get there early so they could watch the local lads assembling the canopy of yellow flowers over the tiny statue at the bend of the road. It wasn't often that they had a chance to meet any men, so the laying of the broom branches was a perfect time to flirt and make friends. They always stopped at the field above the reservoir and sat down by the edge of the bramble and cherry trees that clogged up the edge of the cypress grove to get their shoes out of their paper bags and put them on.

Every time she remembered this, Maria would involuntarily look down at her own shoes, the wide comfortable brown suede shoes that she wore around the house. It seemed strange to her that she should have passed her childhood and girlhood barefoot while now she had a whole row of footwear on the shelf inside her wardrobe. Before, they only wore shoes for the festas, and sometimes, when the share crops were bad and there was nothing over to spare, they had to stay away from the feasts and the dances so as not to shame the family. It had only happened twice, but each time she had sobbed until her mother slapped her. Who would have thought that now she had such a choice of shoes and could go anywhere she pleased and had her own house and a cellar full of wine and ham and more food than she and Beppe could ever eat, she would always stay home and miss the treat.

She stoked the fire and looked across to the brown rexine chair where her brother-in-law sat slumped. Outside there was a rhythmic thud which she knew to be the sound of the chestnut poles being hammered into the ground around the new Madonna. Inside, there was only herself, Tito, her husband's brother and a small thin grey kitten. Maria looked affectionately from the kitten to the man, trying to cast her memory back to how he used to look, all those years ago when he too used to stand on the back of a cart and swing his sledge hammer at the posts, making a frame for the canopy of flowers. He had had an honest body then, strong and full of life and energy, flexing his muscles to the delight of the girls and smiling with the half smile she had grown so fond of.

Tito had always been kind to her. It was he who helped her to carry in the wood, to split the logs when the frost was on the ground and her fingers were slit and bleeding. It was he who helped carry the water from the spring up the hill; he who helped her most with the animals and her chores, with a kind word on his lips and that sweet crooked smile. She looked across the room to him; his mouth was crooked in his sleep, but it had been so for twenty years now, ever since the stroke had grappled him to the ground and kept him there a limp, half-lifeless thing. She tried to remember how he used to be, to compare and keep her old friend in her mind as she toiled with his daily needs. As she lifted him from his bed to the chair and back again, she knew that were he his old self, it would be he who would help her to carry the load. By a cruel twist her helper became the burden. She mopped the dribble from the side of his mouth without a hint of tenderness, then she turned away and called the kitten to her, tickling it affectionately and muttering, 'Dio buono, thank goodness for you, you silly cat, you've got more sense than my poor brother-in-law.'

At first she had nursed him with all the love and gratitude due to one who had eased her own bewildering early days of marriage. But after the first five years, when Tito showed no signs of recovery, she had begun to feel tired by the sheer weight of his almost lifeless body. She kept him alive by spoon-feeding him broth, but where once she had talked to her inert patient, unfolding her hopes and disappointments, she came increasingly to tell him only her woes. She

149

would grumble at him, knowing that he could neither hear nor reply. Often she would tell him how hard it made her life to have to nurse him. She would complain that she could never more go out, not even to the village or the shops. Friends died and she missed their funerals, children were born and she missed their christenings.

When the festa of San Crescentino came round, and everyone gathered on the far side of the valley, she missed that too. Late at night she would lie in bed waiting for her husband to return, drunk from the dance. Through the thick stone wall of her bedroom she could hear Tito snoring his thick rumbling snore while from outside she could hear the strains of violins and accordions playing tangos and polkas under the stars. Maria liked the polka best, she could still feel the music in her feet. There were times when she wanted to get up and get dressed in her best dress and run away from Tito and her servitude and join her sisters and all her friends dancing through the night. There would be wine and hot ciacias baked on flat stones. She was always invited, but she never went; not even to the festa of the Madonna which took place on her doorstep. She could have stepped down from her rows of immaculately tended flowers and vegetables and joined the procession as it passed her house. Don Annibale, the priest was there at the fore and all of the hamlet followed him. As they passed, they waved to her, calling her down, 'Come on, Maria. Come on.'

Tito was her cross, she carried him all year round in her own private procession, so she never joined the others.

There had been many ups and downs over the years with Tito's health, but she had always nursed him through. He himself never showed any signs of knowing whether he was breathing or not. When his temperature rose and he sweated and wheezed, it was only Maria who seemed to feel any pain, not he. His brother, Beppe had always been undemonstrative, yet he cared for his annual pig, and the ducks and chickens in his yard, and he cared for his wife and his brother too, but he could never say so, or even show it beyond the odd grunt or word. In his own way he loved Maria, and he loved her doubly for nursing his brother, but that was something that he always left unsaid. Beppe was a man who felt uncomfortable with words. They had never had any place in his life, you could not grow them or eat them, or so he thought; so he stuck to the crops he knew and, like his wife, whenever he felt overcome by emotion, he took refuge in teasing the cat. They had always had a cat or a kitten about. Beppe had a way with kittens, they would follow him in and out of his cantina, often choosing his tool box as a nest. He would have liked Maria to change her dress and leave her apron and go with him to the festa. He had often hinted as much and even told her, but she refused. Even when her sister offered to babysit Tito, she had insisted in staying herself. Twenty-two years she had nursed him all herself.

Maria had come to think of Tito as immortal. Her own tiredness had reached such proportions that she was convinced that she must die before him. His life consisted of

151

empty hours, bowls of broth, a warm fire and no strain or work to break him. Meanwhile she toiled and drudged, wrapping bits of plastic round her chapped hands to hold down the cracks. She kept the fire stoked all through the year for Tito to sit by. She kept the animals fed and fat, then she slaughtered them. She cooked and washed, pruned and hoed until all her bones ached. She and Beppe were saving. They saved most of what they made. They were saving to stave off the poverty that they both remembered. Things were going well. They had enough money to buy almost anything they wanted, but they didn't buy things on the whole.

Sometimes, in the summer, when the days were longer, Maria used to really pine to be outside. She kept the geraniums on her balcony so well that they trailed down and caught in her visitors' hair when they arrived and called up from under her window.

'Maria!'

Her house would often fill with visitors, and the invitations never ceased.

'We're going to the market on Thursday, why don't you come?'

'There's a cresima at Marcello's on Saturday afternoon, I could come and pick you up.'

'Nunzia will look after Tito, she'd be happy to.'

Maria wouldn't even say no, she would just set her face as she had so many years before against the world and all her pleasure there. Her friends and family knew better than to argue with her. Yet, when she was alone with Tito, she would mumble at him.

'Dio buono, I never get out of this house. You're a prisoner to your illness, and I'm your prisoner. You have kept me in solitary confinement. If only you would speak to me!'

Tito's silence made her want to cry. At times she imagined that he was refusing to speak, at times she tried to make him speak. She knew, at heart, that he was as honest as he had ever been, he wasn't keeping anything back from her, his life was empty and his body, lifeless. A mere look told her so, just as before, a mere look had shown all his fine qualities. Even the crooked smile had assumed the expression of a half-wit.

Every year as the procession wended its way down the hill past her house and past the fields, she stood and watched and yearned to be there. Don Annibale blessed the fields and the villagers chanted. After that, there was the lunch. It never varied in its menu, since the war, it never had. There were three types of crostini, tagliatelli with a meat sauce, spaghetti with funghi, roast meat, salad, fruit salad, coffee, cakes and wine. She could imagine where everyone sat. She could hear them all laughing and talking. The jokes would be the same jokes. The girls would be flirting, the boys would be boasting. If it were not for Tito, she would be there, sitting beside Beppe and her family, passing the big bottles of wine up and down the table. Or she might be one of the servers, since she had made the sauce. She might carry one of the huge dished trays, ladling out plate after plate of pasta.

When Tito died, after twenty-two years of paralysis, Maria could not believe it. She attended his funeral and cleaned out his room, but she could not accept that he wouldn't be back again. When she looked at his empty chair by the kitchen grate, she felt that he must be in his bed, and when she looked at his empty bed, she felt that he must surely still be slumped in the kitchen. She realised that the weariness she had felt at lifting and tending him had actually been a pleasure which she now missed keenly. She no longer knew what to do with her time. The days dragged interminably and, although she complained into the empty corner of the room about it, she could glean no comfort from speaking to the blank wall. Although he had never answered by so much as a nod or a sigh, her words had gone out to a human form and not just to an empty room. She felt so desperate that she tried talking to Beppe, much to his confusion.

Friends and relatives came to share her grief, but no one seemed to understand her loss. They described his death as a blessing, imagining that she must be glad to be relieved of such a weight. She felt the cracks in her hands filling up with loneliness. At night, her pillow exuded solitude; by day every familiar object in her kitchen became strange. She missed Tito and she began to feel guilty for the cross words she had spoken while he was alive. Although one part of her knew full well that Tito had never been able to hear her, she began to believe that he had, and that he had heard her resenting his presence, complaining about all the extra chores his stroke had heaped on her. She would sit staring into the fire and the deserted corner trying to will back all the dio buonos she had sighed over the years.

'Tito,' she would whisper, 'can you hear me? Do you know how much I miss you, how much I loved you, Tito dear?'

She hated the sound of her own voice and the sight of her unoccupied hands. No matter how long she dragged out her daily chores, she had time on her hands. People came to lure her away, but she clung to the past. She observed a year of mourning, wearing only black instead of her usual navy blue and she went nowhere except to the memorial service that was held on the anniversary of his death. May came and went taking with it the festa of the Madonnina, and Maria locked herself away, refusing even to stand on her balcony and watch the procession pass. People said, 'Next year Maria will be with us again.'

They didn't call to her, because they respected the form of her mourning. There were those who thought she had suffered enough during Tito's lifetime, but they didn't say so.

The summer passed with its blistering heat and scorched the hillsides, then the autumn came and the grapes were gathered in and pressed and Beppe's cellar was replenished with a new wine. In November, the chestnuts were gathered and soaked and stored. At New Year, when Maria stayed away from the festa of Capodanne and the fireworks, her family explained, 'She'll be waiting for the festa of la Madonnina, it was always her favourite.'

In January the pigs were killed and the frosts set in. Maria sat in her kitchen with the rows of salamis and cured hams hanging from hooks in the ceiling. The smell of meat made the cat frisky. These were the days, when the land was sleeping and there was little to do on account of the frosts and the rain, when Maria spent most time huddled in her kitchen. The empty chair haunted her. Her visitors watched her and were worried. She was still as hospitable as ever, but she had not recovered from Tito's death. She was locked in her loss.

Finally, May arrived and the preparations began for the festa of the little Madonna. The canopy was made. The cakes were baked. Maria killed geese and chickens to cook their livers for a sauce. The broom flowers were carried down to the bend in the road, leaving a trail of fallen petals all along the dust track that passed her house. The procession began, and Maria was still in her kitchen staring wistfully at Tito's chair. When Don Annibale reached her gate, he paused, and all the village paused behind him. They waited for several minutes, and a couple of women went up to find Maria. They returned without her.

'What happened?' they were asked.

'She has set her face, she won't come down.'

'Dio buono!' came a chorus from her friends.

'Maria!' they called up to her window, 'O, Maria!'

Then Maria came to the small iron work balcony of her kitchen and stood knee-deep between her geraniums and looked down and waved.

156

Don Annibale moved on, blessing the small patch of land where Maria and Beppe grew their vegetables and where Maria grew her flowers. He sprinkled holy water on their strip of land and then continued down the hill to the statue of the Madonnina. Alone on her balcony, Maria stared down at her brown shoes freckled with geranium petals and smiled to herself, recalling her bare feet and the past. Then she watched the procession make its way to the canopied statue and back again, just as she used to do when she was nursing Tito, then she went back into her kitchen and continued to nurse her grief.

Antonio
Mezzanotte

E,very day he wandered around the village gathering information. He could detect the slightest changes and moved instinctively to the source of trouble. He knew when love affairs ended even before the couple involved had officially decided to go their own ways. He knew when a wife cuckolded her husband and with whom. He knew when a husband stopped in the scrublands above the village and kissed one of the local girls in a silent tryst. He knew when families fell out with each other and at what moment a feud began. Like a bird of prey he circled the narrow stone streets, uphill and down, storing gossip in his one good hand.

His presence was so familiar that no one stopped to wonder what he was doing or where he was going. He was just Mezzanotte doing his rounds. At the end of each survey he would pause at the little bar and tobacconist at the top of the hill opposite the church of Santa Maria and lean on the bar and nod to the sound of the approaching barman. It was usually the barman who spoke; Mezzanotte surrounded himself with silence.

'Un cynar?'

Mezzanotte would nod and wait for the drink to be poured and the bottle to be held straight again before adding in his deep urgent voice, 'Abondante.' And the barman would double the thick black liquid in the glass. It was a ritual that happened many times a day, but the communion of the double order was important. Then Mezzanotte would gulp down his bitter drink and smile a wry smile that made the many scars on his face flicker. Then he would nod, touching the bar to steady himself before going out into the street again, and the daylight that had not been daylight for him for nearly fifty years. His hours were a continual darkness since the day when a landmine blew up in his face and seared his eyes from their sockets. A blind man with a plastic arm and a plastic hand and a hundred scars, he felt his way past familiar stones to the small room where he lived.

It was June, it was hot, there were lizards on the walls, and the oak woods rustled already dry leaves in the Umbrian wind. The children were out of school, dodging potential errands, darting between the cool stone walls as they hid from cousins and uncles who might send them to Gelsomino the blacksmith to sharpen a scythe, or the parched tobacco fields to carry drinking water. Experience had taught the village boys to keep under cover and hide their catapults and the battered communal football. It wasn't safe to greet adults in these busy times, yet they greeted Mezzanotte.

'Buona sera, Mezzanotte,' they called after him.

'Sera!' he growled, and smiled, puckering the scar-veins

162

around his mouth. The boys were going to play football, they were making their way in twos and threes to the Campo sportivo. They'd be hardly breathing, hoping to pass through the sun-stained streets unnoticed just as he himself used to do. He smiled again, a broken smile in recognition of his own harmlessness. He was not a threat like other men. He was almost one of them: a big boy suspended in time, clinging on to his youth, pretending to be invisible. He twisted his plastic hand in its socket and continued to edge his way down the hill, patrolling the village, amassing bits of news. He was not a scandalmonger, he did not spread his information, he just liked to gather it and keep it stacked up around him like sand bags against a blast. News that might have seemed colourful if retold at the time, dulled over the years until what Mezzanotte knew acquired the same black-and-whiteness of his world. The specks of colour could have been piles of newsprint chewed by mice; but Mezzanotte was comforted by the staleness of his old news and he needed the constant drip-feed of current affairs. The affairs of his village were all that interested him, the rest of the world had been blotted out by the war.

After months in the Military Hospital in Perugia, they had taken him home to this village where he had been born and where his family and friends had cradled him back to life. The parameters of the parish confines were the boundaries of his world. Like a mule tied to an olive press he turned, round and round, taking note of every movement, word and transaction. He knew the smell and voice of every man and woman in the village. He knew the cycle of every plot of land: when the onions and garlic would be sown, when the tobacco seed would be planted in the covered stone troughs, when the sweet peppers would be planted and when the sunflowers sown. He knew when the five kinds of wild lettuce would spring up in the woods and along the edge of the road, and where they would be most abundant. He knew where the porcini mushrooms grew best and truffles and chanterelles. He never needed a cross-breed dog to sniff such things out of the leaf mould in the hills, his own nose guided him to them, just as it did to the first posy of violets and the wild asparagus.

Antonio Mezzanotte was as much a part of the village as the old poet Silvio with his leather apron and his tiny wizened face, or as Estelio, the organiser, or Alvaro, the butcher. He was as much a part of the village as Rosina and Maria who cooked the pasta for the village festas, and as Menchina who served behind the bar with a strip of green ribbon tied round her head on all the days when she had migraines. No one ever suffered alone here, however much they suffered, there was always help and company. Not even the war had changed the spirit of the village, the give and take. They had stood together against the Germans and the Moroccans and the Fascists alike, locked in their time warp. Relatively few bombs had fallen near them, and few mines had exploded. What casualties there had been were nursed so that like Mezzanotte himself they became a part of everything.

Yet all the other casualties had died, one by one. There

were no other war invalids left like him whose hand and eyes were scattered somewhere in the hills. The wounded soldiers died. And Mezzanotte's family had died: his mother – who never recovered from seeing her broken child brought home on a stretcher with his face embroidered with scars like one of her woven table mats gone wrong – and his father, his brother, his cousins, his aunts and uncles, every one of them had died; only Mezzanotte had lingered on, patrolling round and round from the campo santo where they lay in illuminated concrete drawers, to the bar at the top of the hill and the bar at the bottom of the hill, past the new houses and the two churches – one for masses and one for functions. The village was his surrogate family now. They accepted him as he was – broken.

It was June again, and the acacia was drifting its scented petals through the hot afternoon. It was in June that all the village wound itself up into a fervour to celebrate the festival of San Crescentino. It was in June that Mezzanotte had been blown apart, the June of 1946. Antonio Mezzanotte was eleven years old, born in 1935, Gregorio was twelve. Everything was being made ready then. The trestles were stacked against the side of the church, faggots of wood were lying in neat piles to heat the bread ovens and grill the meat. The village pots, the massive cast iron cauldrons that could hold enough pasta for 400 people, were oiled and standing by. All the Partisans who had survived the fighting had come home. They had been thin and hollow-eyed the year before, but now they had filled out. Together with the fugitives and the soldiers, the chickens and the pigeons had come home to roost. Grain and wine that had been stashed and buried for years had been restored to their rightful cantinas. This was to be a festa of plenty and of independence and survival. Everyone in the village and in the outlying hamlets was contributing, either with food or help. All the children were helping too. Antonio Mezzanotte and his best friend, Gregorio, had been sighted in the woods and if anyone could find more porcini, it would be Antonio and Gregorio, they had a knack for knowing where the most succulent funghi would be hiding.

They went past the vineyards and the olive groves that hemmed the village on its way to Sant Agnese and the oak woods beyond. This was their day of reconnoitre, they must find the porcini and mark them for the following day, allowing them to grow in size and be as fresh as possible for the festa. From the crest of the hill they rounded down into the gnarled chestnut grove that knuckled its way down the slope under the guard of the sentinel cypresses that grew along the ridge. Below, they could see a huddle of old women with their long skirts hitched between their thighs and coloured scarves tightly knotted round their hair. They were seated around a huge pot hung over a campfire. Half of them were strangling ducks and geese, the other half were gutting them. A smell of singed feathers wafted up the hill. Soon the honey-scented acacia blossom was blending in the air with the honey of the day's baking. Sugar was still scarce, but the chestnut flour mixed well with the local honey. Shot through this almost cloying heaviness was the bitter smell of burning flesh and plume.

It had been surprisingly easy to find the funghi, so Antonio and his friend had the whole afternoon and on till dusk to lie in the sun filtered through chestnut leaves and watch the excitement below. Gregorio said it seemed as though their village were a nest of ants that some unthinking child had kicked open. The ferrying and the hurrying was so great that just watching it made the two boys feel tired. They slept through the afternoon, waking now to a pungent new smell and now to another. They could tell that the giblets were being cooked with the goose livers, rosemary, sage, celery, oil and garlic to make the paste that would be spread on their crostini. They could tell when half of the stock was strained off and mixed with onions and tomatoes and parsley to start the sauce for the first round of tagliatelli. Their own pockets were full of small dark truffles that they had dug out of the roots of chestnut trees. It really wasn't their job to provide the truffles. Giacomo and some of the other men had gone out with their sniffer dogs and brought those in already.

Antonio and Gregorio were up at dawn next day with their reed baskets lined with ferns and full of porcini mushrooms to present to the cooks. They knew that they had done well and the day was theirs to celebrate with the men and not just with the other children. The trestles were assembled and the long benches placed, the garlands of wild flowers and the jugs of wine were all ready. Streams of people were gathering from the outlying crofts. All the children were as scrubbed and clean as Antonio himself. Even the children that lived in the dell under Zeno Poggio like gypsies had made token efforts to tidy themselves up. Even old Piero, who pissed in his pants and never had a good word to say about anyone, had changed his trousers. Antonio's mother had scraped out the earth and mushroom-gills from under his square nails, and his chestnut hair had been shorn so that he looked like a diminutive conscript.

Course followed course: there were antipasti, salami, crostini, thick tagliatelli with a rich ragu, then there was the best tagliatelli bunched and cut by the most skilful pasta cutters in the neighbourhood, covered in slivers of fresh porcini and the smother of grated truffles. When the cooks brought over the cauldron supported by a chain hanging from a chestnut stake, the villagers applauded. Antonio and Gregorio basked in their praise. The truffles were so good that tears came to the eyes of some of the feasters. The carpenter's sons, whom Antonio hated, grunted approval despite themselves.

'Such truffles are scarce this year,' one of the old men said to his brother.

'It was the snow melting so suddenly, it soaked everything. I'd give a lot to know where there were a few truffles left. My dogs can't locate them.'

'Nor mine,' chimed in another.

'But I know where there are truffles,' Antonio piped up.

'Eh, si, eh!' a chorus of men derided him.

'I do, we found them when we were getting the porcini, didn't we Gregorio?'

'It's true,' his friend assured them with his mouth bulging with oily pasta. 'I brought some down for my nonno, I swear by the Madonna . . . I'll bring you one, two . . . and you,' he said, carried away by his own generosity, 'and there were lots, really, dozens; I'll bring them down for all of you and then you can have such pasta again.'

The black wine was flowing freely and the men and boys were already red-faced, their wives and sisters less so, but catching up. Maurizio Poesini had smuggled an entire litre of red wine down his own throat and been carried away in a dead faint. The men winked at each other and nodded towards Gregorio and laughed.

'Here's to them,' someone toasted, and the truffles were forgotten under the general level of shouting and merriment.

The banquet continued until after five o'clock. There were two accordion players fingering up their squeeze boxes under the trees. The worst of the heat was over. The afternoon buzzed with a chorus of snores. There would be tournaments, bocce and briscola, cheese throwing and running races for the boys. In the evening there would be dancing. At midnight, the three fireworks donated by the big house would be let off under the stars and then supper of ciacca stuffed with sausages. The dancing would continue through the night. Infants slept where they fell like soldiers in a littered field.

Every moment of the festa was engraved on Mezzanotte's mind. It was as though his life before had all been distilled into that one brief spell. It was late the next morning when he awoke, still bloated from the feasting and tired by his late night. Gregorio was calling him. Gregorio never seemed to need much sleep, he didn't like sleeping. They had an appointment to go and get the truffles from the hill. They took their truffle picks with them and a piece of cloth to wrap the special earthy balls in.

It was easy to find the spot, and Antonio's nose again confirmed that there were rich pickings under the soil. They dug out one and then another and placed them carefully in the cloth. Truffles were valuable, very valuable, they could sell these in Castello for a small fortune, but instead they would present them to the village elders to thank them for the festa. One each would mean seven truffles, two each would be fourteen. Well, seven would be good enough; but there only seemed to be two. The others must be hidden deeper. They began to scrabble and dig. The smell was there in every grain of soil, the cloying aromatic smell of truffles. They were both digging when the entire festa condensed into a split second and exploded inside Antonio's head.

In Perugia, in the hospital ward, locked in darkness and inexplicable pain, he found himself unable to die. Because he had lived through the war, he had seen how even in his quiet village people died so often that the campo santo was forever filling with mourners. Yet he could neither die nor sleep. Occasionally, like a frail thread joining him to his once known world, a voice from the village would gently pull him back to the brink of comfort. He didn't know he was blind or that he had lost an arm until after he was taken home. It was hard for him to understand such things, it struck him as a kind of carelessness. Why had he been brought home without his hand and his eyes? Where were they? And where was Gregorio? Why did he never come to visit him?

When they told Antonio that his friend was dead, he couldn't take it in. They had been together, gone through the explosion together, so how could Gregorio not be there somewhere suffering like him? He has gone to rest, they told him, to sleep forever with the angels. Surely they knew that Gregorio didn't like sleeping! And why did they keep pressing such weights over his own eyes? It was driving him mad, he ripped at his bandages moving the hand he had and the hand he missed.

He coined his own nickname. Every time boys, or friends of the family came to sit with him, he tried to explain what he felt like and all he could think of was midnight. He said it so often that it stuck: Mezzanotte.

Half a century had passed since then, most of the people present at the time of his own explosion had died. The village had changed, but the festa remained the same. The advent of tobacco had shaken off the mantle of poverty that had kept all Umbria with its face in the dirt since time began. There was a general prosperity. Where once many of the villagers went to the festa to eat, to feast after months of near hunger, it was now a thanksgiving for all their good fortune and a renewal of a vow. It was a communal promise to stand by each other no matter what. No one must miss the festa. Ancient men with transparent skin were there, giving thanks for another year of their frail life. Mezzanotte was not the only armless man. There was many a stone mason or carpenter who had lost varying degrees of fingers and hands who turned out in their Sunday best to break bread with whatever fingers they had left. Nor was he the only villager who was blind. There were three others, including Gregorio's aunt, who lived in darkness.

How could Mezzanotte ever explain the dread he felt at the coming of June? It filled his nights with fear and his days with bitterness. June dredged up the smells and tastes of San Crescentino. All rich food was irrevocably mixed with loss and pain. When he mopped the deep brown gravy from his roast beef, it seemed to be his own blood he tasted. When he swallowed the tagliatelli with slivers of porcini, it was bits of his own face choking down his throat. The shards of bone in the roast were his bones. The smell of truffles moving towards him in its cloud of aromatic steam brought back all that he struggled to forget.

He had passed by the campo santo and San Crescentino with its bell tower squatting over its patched roof. He had taken the slip road past the small vineyard behind the tobacco sheds and he was feeling his way back to the bar at the bottom of the hill. Menchina would be serving. He could still remember her smile from the days when he went in and took water out to the croppers in the fields. There was a slight wind today, despite the summer heat, so Menchina would be wearing her headscarf: the wind was bad for heads. It was bad for his own head, it made his scars ache and it lodged stray memories where they were not wanted.

Along the edge of the road there were pollarded willows. Every year the men lopped off their new growth, using the branches to stake their vines and their tomatoes. Every year the poor gnarled trees grew back, pushing out a prodigious annual growth, and every year the men came with their saws and amputated them back to weeping stumps. The month of June pollarded Mezzanotte's wounds. It reopened all his scars: it lopped off his arm again, it reblasted his sight. Then, every year, he gathered his broken bits and mended them, patching together all that life meant to him, glueing himself back into shape with the human mortar of news.

He had reached the bar, he counted the steps and went in. He drank cynar because he loved the bitterness. It bore no relation to the rich foods of his youth. Wine, brandy, grappa, they all made him want to weep, but the bitter black juice of the artichoke suited him well.

'Buona sera.'

'Sera, Menchina.'

'Un cynar?'

Mezzanotte nodded and then waited until he heard the thick glass being pushed across the counter to him. 'Abondante,' he said.

She'll be coming
round the mountain
when she comes

There was a frost gathering force again, a deep hard frost biting into the ground and glazing every twig and leaf, making them signal to the moonlight. In another couple of hours it would be so thick that it would make footprints as clear as snow. In another couple of hours it would be so cold it wouldn't be worth trying to hide out anymore in the forest. There were no caves and little natural shelter. A solitary, freezing man was stumbling through the woods.

'What a way to die,' he murmured.

The night was unnaturally still around him, even the owls had stopped calling to each other. He was wrapped up in the remains of his torn parachute. He had not eaten for three days. He had found nothing to eat in the woods except for a few raw chestnuts. He wished he had gathered more of them when he could, for the gnarled chestnut groves where he had baled out had given way to oak and pine woods with nothing but insects to offer him. He wondered how cold and tired and hungry a man had to get before he would eat grubs and ants. He pulled the sheets of silk more tightly around his head and shoulders, thankful to them for saving him from a supper of slimy wood lice. He could have sworn they had seen a village before he jumped; a small stone Umbrian village nestling in the rocks. He knew he should have reached it by now. He felt that he would die soon if he didn't reach it, his ribs were cracked and sore with the cold. His face and hands were lacerated from his fall. It was his third day behind the enemy lines, so he would probably die soon anyway. A German patrol would find him and that would be that.

Somewhere in the distance he could swear he heard a sheep bleating. He leant against a tree to listen better; the wind was bleating too. Somewhere behind him something stirred and there was a rustle and a crack. He gripped the tree to steady himself and then froze. Time refused to pass. A drop of cold sweat filled the dip above his lip and then rolled to the ground. He closed his eyes and tensed every muscle in his body ready to take the hail of bullets that he felt must surely follow the splash. He was so afraid that it was a long time before he could move. There was nobody there. He was alone with the night and all his fears. He had always been afraid. It was ridiculous that he should be there at all. He silently cursed the moment when he had decided to study Italian; but for that, he would still be back in England flying missions from the safety of his plane. Every night he would be drinking watery gin with his friends in the mess at Mildenhall. Now it was so cold, and he was tired and confused. Why had he volunteered to do this reconnaissance, and why had he had to jump out here in the middle of nowhere instead of where he was meant to be, 22 miles due south of Rome?

The morning was so cold that Menchina Gambi and her sister, Rosa, could not concentrate on their chores. They had been sent out to gather kindling for the stove; instead, they were playing in the glistening frost, running and sliding to keep warm. Together they found the body of the English airman wrapped in a frosted sheet like a giant slug. Since Menchina was nine and the elder of the two, it was she who got to break the news.

'There's a dead man on the woodpile!' she shouted, in dialect. Within minutes a posse of men and women had gathered to follow her back to the corpse. There was pushing and jostling to get ahead at the front, and much reluctance and hanging back behind. There were those who felt that the body must be dear to them and wanted to see it fast, and there were those who believed the same thing but hoped to postpone the recognition. One or two of the women were already crying. If a body was brought back to Volterrano it must be because it was one of theirs. In such a small village they all knew each other and were somehow related, so here was a cause to weep whoever the dead man turned out to be.

It was Menchina's father who examined the body. It was his woodpile.

'E un inglese,' he said, then he slipped into the dialect they all spoke, the thick unintelligible tongue that had so helped them under the German occupation.

'And this one isn't dead, either . . . Give me a hand some of you. Get back to your houses, let's make this look a bit more natural, eh, there'll be no funerals, so get back to

179

your baking all you women. Come on, some of you men, Roberto Pietro get his legs and help me into the house. Maybe the heat will thaw his tongue.'

His name was Michael, and he was there in Volterrano by mistake. Although he had fallen at random from the sky, dropping down on to the old frontier post of the Papal States, he could not have chosen a safer hiding place. The village had long been hiding Partisans, and many of the cottages and barns had false walls and concealed pits in the floors where a man could hide quite comfortably for weeks on end. Michael sent a message back to Rome via a messenger from the village who carried it into the hills. It was weeks before he received an answer. His instructions were to wait. Someone would contact him, an American, meanwhile he was to wait where he was, keeping a low profile. At first he slept most of the time. He was in the grip of a high fever. Menchina's mother used poultices and herbal teas to cure him. Her father bandaged him with strips of his own parachute. There was an argument the night he did that. Her mother and aunt wanted the silk kept. They said it was a shame to spoil such good stuff. But her father pointed out that there were yards and yards of it and the rest would still be good for dresses and there was nothing they could do with it anyway until the war was over because the Germans might be stupid but they weren't so stupid that they wouldn't notice if all the women of Volterrano started parading around in cream silk dresses instead of their usual rags and aprons. While Michael slept, the rest of his parachute was sealed in an empty biscuit tin and buried deep in the woods.

Lots of the local girls were excited by the thought of all the silk. They spent their evenings discussing just what they would do with their bit of it, if they got a bit. Menchina didn't care for dresses very much, she preferred talking to Michael about all the places he had seen. He could make a rabbit with long ears out of his handkerchief, and he could twist his hands so as to make patterns on the wall when it was dark. As soon as Michael was well enough to leave the house, and once the frosts had eased into the early spring, Michael lived out in the barn. Menchina's father wanted him to stay in their house. There was an attic where he could hide if any soldiers came around, and a trap door gave access to a good hiding place up there should there be a proper house-to-house search. Michael had insisted on living out. He kept telling them, 'I shouldn't even be here, you know there could be a reprisal if I'm found. At least let me stay outside where you can claim that you've never seen me before if I do get caught.'

He worried about the children, about Menchina and Rosa who carried him his food. He wanted to leave, but he didn't know where to go without the help of the Partisans, and they were mostly away fighting elsewhere. Not much of the war had come to Volterrano. From time to time messages got back to him, always telling him to wait.

Every day the local children took their frayed books and went to school walking along the unmade road to the next village. Volterrano was a dead end, beyond it were the woods of Tuscany. Every week some of the men went to market, and once a month a group of villagers set off at four o'clock in the morning to walk the five hours to Castiglion Fiorentino to trade there, but no one ever came to take the hidden airman away. Michael was the pride of Volterrano, a secret that the entire village shared and kept.

Michael stayed there all through the summer of 1943. It was his second summer with the village which had come to feel more and more like home. His own village of Chagford began to feel almost unreal. His parents, the neighbours, the grammar school in Exeter, the airbase in Mildenhall and even his friends all became secondary to the affairs of Volterrano. His new family, the Gambis, all complained at the lack of real flour, but Michael grew to love the bitter taste of the chestnut bread they ate. It reminded him of the mouthfuls of raw chestnuts he had swallowed when he came to, wounded in the woods. It reminded him of how lucky he was to be sheltered by such enveloping kindness.

The summer was so hot that by August the oak leaves were already tarnished and the slightest breeze rustled them into the scorched grass. School finished early in June and all through the holidays Menchina and her friends took Michael with them into the woods to gather mushrooms, blackberries, birds' eggs and anything else to eat. A pair of peregrine falcons was nesting somewhere in the rocks above San Martin and they circled over the woods and the village, hovering. Whenever Michael laid back to rest, he would see them, and he began to feel as superstitious as the villagers. The birds of prey were warning him to leave. As the summer shifted into autumn, he began to fear more and more for the village. An instinct in him made him want to stay and fight and protect those people whom he had come to love, but reason told him that their greatest risk lay with him and he should leave.

In September, when the regional leader of the Partisans returned, Michael sent word to him that he was going to try to make his way to Switzerland and then back to England. He was told to wait. The Allies were on their way. It would not be long. All through the winter he was restless. Food was scarce and the frosts pinched and shrivelled everyone. The oldest and the youngest were culled by want, and the graveyard filled. Three times, patrols of Germans came into the village, but each time the look-out boys gave the alarm and Michael was safely hidden by the time the soldiers arrived.

Michael had been in the village long enough to know how low the food supplies had sunk. The stashes of grain, rice and dried meat that had eked out the earlier years of the war were all but exhausted. The winter would be a hungry one and, if for any reason the Allies did not arrive in time, he doubted whether this particular village could survive the next winter after that. When he remembered how short supplies had been even in Exeter in the years before he was dropped, he wondered if the advent of the Allies would actually alleviate the famine he dreaded.

In the spring of 1944 the reprisals began. A father and son were taken out of their house and shot on the road to

Mucignano. Two weeks later, on the day before Palm Sunday, a boy was shot at Petrelle. Michael and some of the other villagers heard the shot. People began to disappear. Every night the villagers shared their beds with fear. Sounds which had never bothered anyone now caused nightmares and muffled cries. Michael made up his mind to leave. The days were growing warm and long again. The Allies had landed and were moving up towards them. The Germans were nervous and trigger happy. The spot-checks and patrols increased and the disappearances continued.

Every day, Michael waited for Menchina to return home from school, then he told her and her friends to follow him up into the woods. When he reached the part where he knew there was an acoustic dip, he told them, 'Listen, the Allies are on their way, and I'll have to go soon and join them. Whatever happens, I'll be back once the war is over. You know that . . . I'm coming back to live here in Volterrano. I'd like to stay and explain to our side how much you have helped me, but I have to go back and fight. I'm teaching you this song, so that when you see them coming and you know it's the English or the Yanks, all you children must stand up and sing it. Then they'll know, and they'll help you and help your parents.'

Day after day he persisted, lecturing the children in their native dialect and then teaching them, in English:

She'll be coming round the mountain when she comes
She'll be coming round the mountain when she comes.

It took much longer than he thought. The falcons were circling above them as though to show the Germans where they were. Menchina and some of the older children learnt the words, while the younger ones joined in with the chorus, 'Singing ay ay yippie yippie ay.'

When, early one morning in May, Menchina woke and took Michael's barley coffee to him in the bar, and found him gone, she was humming the tune under her breath. For days and weeks after he had gone the children practised it, hoping to chant him back into their midst. He had left a note to say that he was leaving because of the children. He feared discovery and a reprisal. He promised to write as soon as he was safe.

Eight weeks later, the Allies came, marching down the road from Castiglion Fiorentino. The children of Volterrano stood on the ledge of sheer rock above the road as they had been instructed, and they sang their song. The sound of the tanks and the marching and talking drowned it out, and the troops were in a hurry to join battle further on. So the war passed and no one heard them. Long after the war ended, they were still waiting for Michael. The children grew up and married and had children of their own, yet no word ever arrived from Michael. Not even the postcard he had promised to say he was safe. So they never knew whether he had died or simply forgotten them. Menchina and her friends never forgot him, though. They remembered how he used to make tea out of bits of burnt toast, and rabbits' ears out of cloth. They remembered how concerned he had always been, not that the Germans would shoot him, but that they would hurt the Gambis for harbouring him. An entire family had been shot somewhere in the hills beyond Ansina for helping a Partisan. The news had reached Volterrano the day before Michael left. They remembered his mop of straw-like hair that had merged so naturally into the straw of the Gambis' barn, and his summer sunburn which stood out so dangerously on his face. But most of all, whenever there was an occasion when a group of them would gather together, they remembered his song. The chorus had become a part of their dialect 'Singingayayyippie yippie ay.'

Only Menchina believed he would return. She never gave up hope. After the British and the Americans and the Moroccans had marched along the track from Castiglion Fiorentino to Volterrano and on northwards, the road was opened up and thousands of others passed through in their wake. Menchina saw them all, coming round the mountain, and she knew that one of them would be him. The rest of the village had given up waiting for him long since, they wouldn't even recognise Signor Gambi's boy, and Signor Gambi himself was dead. But Menchina knew that she would recognise Michael, he'd be wearing silk pyjamas when he came, pale parachute silk pyjamas like he did before.